Published by Semiotext(e)
PO BOX 629, South Pasadena, CA 91031
www.semiotexte.com

Cover Photograph by Sasha Frere-Jones
Cover Design: Lauren Mackler
Layout: Hedi El Kholti

ISBN: 978-1-63590-196-2

Distributed by the MIT Press, Cambridge, MA.
Printed and bound in the United States of America.

Sasha Frere-Jones
Earlier

Semiotext(e)

For Deborah,

the first and last person to tell me to write this

The Trees on South Portland (1978)

The plane trees go across the cars. The streetlights are twenty feet up. The rain is heavy and not loud. I should be in bed. The rain is heavy and the street is quiet. The storm covers the trees. All plants move toward the sun. All the trees point to the middle of the street. Where is the sun?

The Russian (1967)

An hour after I am born, they call me Alexander. Every time I am told this, it is pointed out that an hour goes by between these events. The next day, my English mother's English mother tells my parents to call me Sasha. It is the Russian familiar, a way of saying "Alex" in a different language. We need these nicknames because a bunch of men on the English side—the Frere side—are named Alexander. Every Alexander is called something else: Dids, Toby, Harry. My grandmother thinks *Alex* is too boring, so I get *Sasha*. She is always right, so I simply accept all of it when I am old enough to process any of it. Or, most of it—I never get used to the Toby-and-Harry thing. It's like the English and pudding. Any sweet food can be pudding and any name can be melted into whatever you need it to mean. It doesn't seem right.

The Frere family name is not French now but it was definitely French around 1066.

I begin as an American Jones with a Russian first name. The hyphen and the not-French French come later. My parents transliterate the Russian as *Sascha* for the first few months of my life and then drop the *c*.

Pepsi Bottle (1977)

I'm out for two weeks with chicken pox. When I come back to Packer Day Camp, I win the floor-hockey goal competition, fifty-two goals to Danny O'Halloran and his fifty-one. My trophy is a two-liter glass bottle of Pepsi wrapped in a Styrofoam sleeve covered with logos and ingredients. The bottle disappears. I keep the sleeve. The comments are still there, pushed into the foam by pencil. Between "Have a good summer" and "Stay in touch" is Danny's handwriting, distressed enough that he may have started with something else and rubbed it out before arriving at a conclusion: "You suck."

The Curls (1981)

There's only one photograph of my father in our house. It hangs downstairs at 28 Old Fulton Street. It's sepia and it seems to be a hundred years old. The technology and mood are Victorian. It's my father, as a boy, looking adorable, smiling quietly with a high forehead and tight curls. He looks like my Sam, happy, and maybe from another planet, not because of how he looks or any apparent state of mind but because the source and the event are from a period my father never mentioned. My father did not ever talk about his childhood.

Decades later, when I'm a father and Jonah is doing a family-tree project for Hebrew school, he discovers that my grandfather, Roger Jones, was born in Tuscaloosa in 1900 and had ten brothers. I can imagine the conversations in that house. I want to know how this would have affected my father before he was even able to understand conversations.

Roger loved golf, so we live with a silver trophy he won in a tourney. It is kept in a tall piece of dark wooden furniture that displays objects and gives harbor to big holiday dishes down below. My grandfather dies when I am five, a few months after his wife Augusta passes. If I met them, I have no memory of it.

Intentionality (2023)

I remember writing *The Mouse Who Lived at A&S* when I was seven. I remember wanting to be in a band when I was nine. I remember my mom making me a Tribble and staining the fake fur with coffee to make it look right. I remember seeing the spray-painted marks left by surveyors in the grass and following them like I was one of the Hardy Boys. I remember eating chop suey out of a can on a Thursday night while my parents were practicing with the choir at Lafayette Avenue Presbyterian Church. I remember my parents having Beatles albums even though they had no other popular music. I remember my dad bringing home three Moog albums from the *Stereo Review* discard pile. I remember playing "Johnny B. Goode" in the gymnasium at church in my mother's most sparkly shirt. I remember our pastor looming above me with his strawberry face and hissing at me about liking music more than the Bible and me saying "Eat a bug" and running downstairs to play pool. I remember going to Gage & Tollner for my birthday and wondering if it was actually like that in the nineteenth century. I remember buying Foreigner's "Cold as Ice" instead of the Brothers Johnson's "Strawberry Letter 23" because I didn't know which song the radio DJ was referring to. I remember throwing a garbage bag full of water off a roof on Clermont with James Hoins and watching it hit the only parked car on the whole block and learning it was his dad's. I remember Barbara asking me out in sixth grade while I was waiting to take a free throw in the gym and saying no because I thought she was making fun of me. I remember making a Heathkit radio with my dad and how the solder smelled when it pooled around the resistor. I remember smoking my first menthol cigarette with James. I remember smoking my last menthol cigarette with James. I remember the off-beat clicking of the fare box on the B38 and the pause between lights as the undercarriage of the bus rose above the potholes of Tillary. I remember my dad cooking his version of Chinese food and crying to opera on Saturdays. I remember the people who would put sign-language cards on everyone's knee in a subway car and then come back through collecting the cards unless somebody bought one but nobody ever did. I remember starting a vocabulary list with John Cullum and adding new words to an onionskin sheet with the typewriter and thinking I should read Pynchon since all of his words seemed to come from *Gravity's Rainbow*. I remember winning the first Bad Brains ROIR tape from WNYU and it taking weeks and weeks to arrive in the mail. I remember being a messenger in the summer of 1983 and listening to Crash Crew on my Walkman and hoping I would get a delivery on the West Side or Queens so I could take the F and get some AC. I remember buying *Bits & Pieces* by Big Apple Production and wondering if they were in the Yellow Pages. I remember wanting to write more plays and be in more plays. I remember going to the weed bodega on Myrtle and seeing the single roll of Charmin in the window right next to the single box of Kellogg's Corn Flakes. I remember buying *Taking Tiger Mountain* and *Exile on Main Street* at the same store on Fifth Avenue near Forty-Second Street and being confused and delighted by both and not being 100 percent sure I liked weird old-people music as much as disco. I remember going with my family to Philadelphia and buying the first Specials album, the first Pretenders album, and Gary Numan's *The Pleasure Principle* and sitting in a Holiday Inn and wanting very much to get back to Brooklyn. I remember worrying that not being in a band during high school meant I would never be in one. I remember going to visit my dad's work friends and hearing both Edgar Froese's *Aqua* and Eno's *Ambient 1* and being terrified by how good the music felt. I remember listening to the B-52's and Buzzcocks and Wire at Ben's house and wishing his hot older sister would come home. I remember John playing me *Brain Salad Surgery* in his room and being jealous of his nice stereo and also wanting to love the album as much as he did. I remember writing J-cards for my mixtapes with a Rapidograph and struggling to get the uprights of HAIRCUT 100 all smooth and even. I remember buying Paul Winley's *Super Disco Brake's* on Fulton Street and being pissed at how bad the pressings were. I remember my dad's work friends sneaking me into the Ritz to see the Specials and thinking their underwater sleepwalk music was magical and that small clubs were a lot better than hockey rinks. I remember hearing "Somebody Else's Guy" on the radio all year long and hoping every time it wouldn't be the version with the terrible rapper. I remember ending high school and assuming theater would be my future. I remember trying to put on Pinter's *The Birthday Party* with Karla Schickele but students couldn't book the theater and do their own plays. I remember sitting on red stairs in the lobby with Dara and wishing I could turn eighteen during high school instead of after. I remember leaving the Rock Hotel after the senior dance when I was a junior and making out with Krisztina and thinking, "Ah yes adulthood has begun I should make business cards." I remember typing up all of the Velvet Underground's lyrics on my dad's IBM Selectric. I remember going to the emergency room in Providence with a Cornish game hen bone in my throat and telling the nurse I loved her after she gave me intravenous valium. I remember Butthole Surfers playing at 6:00 p.m. just to confuse people and being grateful someone at the Living Room tipped us off. I remember someone writing that Kool G Rap and Kane and Rakim were equally important contemporaries and thinking, "No, that's wrong" and wondering if I should write about it. I remember Deborah coming to my apartment in Brooklyn for this first and only time and saying the traffic on Flatbush was too loud but she liked the potpourri I put in the bathroom. I remember Deborah telling me about the summer she lived with Madonna and how Madonna never refilled the ice trays. I remember listening to *Excursions in Ambience* in the loft with no heat and seeing my breath while I made the big signs that said WILL YOU and MARRY ME and then hung them from the ceiling in the back room. I remember listening to the Grifters and drinking champagne in our nightgowns the day after we got married. I remember writing my very first pieces for a zine and not thinking it was weird that my editor called me at noon and yelled at me even though it was the best time to talk and then finding out she'd been on heroin the whole time. I remember going to an older rock critic's house and him calling me a "pamphleteer" because he thought I was writing about my friends even though I did not know Roni Size and Aceyalone personally. I remember Deborah imitating Mary's Australian accent and saying, "There are lovely noodles on the balcony." I remember sitting in the Civic and listening to the tape called '99 and hearing Damien Jurado's "Honey Baby" with Sam in the car seat and feeling as full as a person can feel with some kind of water running through me as we sat and rattled. I remember asking our tour manager why the cars in Rome all had dents in the back and him saying, "When we stop, we kiss the car." I remember being a judge at the DMC Finals and feeling deeply unqualified to be judging a turntable competition of any kind. I remember being tired and scared at the Paradiso and then turning on the amp and smelling the tubes kick in. I remember playing a gig at the Roundhouse in London, a club full of people who loved us, and striking our gear and coming back to an empty room because of some cabaret law. I remember the military police in St. Petersburg asking me over and over "Drugs? Guns? Drugs? Guns?" and then giving me my passport back and speaking English out of nowhere. I remember going to see Bob Dylan in Washington, DC, with John Bennet and watching him pull a Bible-sized brick of cash out of the trunk because he maybe might I don't know buy a guitar. I remember Deborah's father, Doug, getting sick and finally teaching me how to put up drywall because there wouldn't be another chance to pretend he couldn't. I remember the woman who lived in China writing "I fell in love" on her blog instead of telling me directly and then showing up at my apartment. I remember when the rock star assumed I was a woman and wrote to me and mocked my name. I remember doing a reading in Chicago and thinking it might be time to get sober because I'd volunteered to read Burroughs without remembering I don't like Burroughs. I remember falling asleep in the first half of roughly twenty movies on the couch with a sandwich from a place that rarely made sandwiches. I remember my new boss asking me if I knew the band who played the Bataclan and could I talk to them "as friends." I remember the nice doctor at NYU Langone asking if I wanted to go to the psych ward and me saying yes even though I meant to say no. I remember seeing Deborah on the lawn in Connecticut sitting on the same spot where we got married twenty-six years earlier wearing her second wedding dress and looking infinitely more beautiful than she did the first time. I remember looping through the Financial District on my bike during the pandemic and missing my dad and Deborah and wondering if delivery guys cry whenever they want because they're always alone.

The Golf Ball (1985)

One of my friends in freshman year is Juan Doubrechat, a kid from Poughkeepsie. We establish a connection at the end of the second semester, almost certainly induced by a common need to find housing. True to type, I don't think about where I will live until the last minute. Juan is maybe a friend of the freckle-faced girl across the hall who always has snacks.

Juan and I dance at a few frat parties, because there are, it turns out, a few fraternities that host decent parties at Brown. One night, while the DJ is playing "How Soon Is Now?" and then Bronski Beat's "Smalltown Boy," I turn to see Juan smiling and tracing triangles in the air. I don't know what to do so I just laugh and clap. We have planned to be roommates in Spanish House, an off-campus apartment building that we somehow qualify for. I speak Spanish (badly) and maybe Juan studies Spanish?

My sophomore year is uncut aimlessness. I am in the Semiotics Department but I'm not yet making a film. I've ended up forming a band called Bad Timing but we're a little confusing, and unbearable when I sing. We do a good version of "Waiting for the Man," which is the only song I can perform without sounding unsuited to the task. Our guitarist, Galen Wade, has lots of effects pedals that he's really good at using. He loves U2 and the Cocteau Twins and I get stoned in his room in Pembroke. Miguel Lawson is our drummer, a Cali-sounding kid whose family is Bahá'í. He loves fusion and plays incredibly well. I write and sing a terrible song called "Back Wave." My idea is something like Echo & the Bunnymen but I sound queasy.

Juan is never in our room because he's always at his boyfriend Jerry's house, an actual off-campus apartment rather than a dorm room. I listen to Minutemen's *My First Bells* cassette and the Cure's *The Head on the Door*, along with a mix my friend John makes me of free jazz and the Pop Group. When Juan is around, he listens to my Cure cassette, absconding with it as needed. I'm happy he's found someone but I am childishly mad at the world. I have few friends and no girlfriend and no focus.

The moment in my freshman year that gives me something to hold on to, before I slide into a ditch, is taking Semiotics 12 with Mary Ann Doane. Other than studying with Joe Flaherty and Nancy Fales-Garrett at St. Ann's, this is the most important thing that happens to me on the grounds of a school. I come very close to not taking the class. I end up in Semiotics 12 only because I run into somebody the day I give up on theater. I leave a terrible audition, at sea and flimsy, and walk to the arch on the main quad where course listings are posted. I must look miserable because a slightly older student looks at me and says, "What's going on?" Theater has failed me, blah blah blah, woe is me, I want to make things and think—I say something melodramatic like that. He tells me to take Semiotics 12. I'll read great stuff and see movies and, maybe, eventually, I can make my own film.

"Maybe I'll be your TA."

He was, and his name is Todd Haynes. We write single-page papers with no margins or line spacing, making them closer to three pages long. Todd likes my writing and encourages me to continue. On Monday and Tuesday night, there are screenings. That year, the lineup is untouchable: *Sans Soleil, Wavelength, Jeanne Dielman, 23, Quai du Commerce, 1080 Bruxelles, Bad Timing, Alphaville.* I read Barthes, the cherry on top.

Memories of this hold me while I accomplish nothing and sulk for all of first semester, waiting for Leslie Thornton's film class in second semester of sophomore year. I am trying to understand my anxiety, which is not a water-cooler topic in 1985. My term for anxiety is *the Golf Ball*, because it seems like a thing that could only be hidden with difficulty. It is going to be either visible or felt, never eliminated. Wherever you stash it, you will sense it.

The Bowlcut + The Bolex (1986)

Leslie wears black jackets, maybe silk, maybe the Mao style? She is still and quiet, a steady presence who patiently explains the Bolex to us. A woman named Amy is in this class, as is Doug Liman. Amy goes on to spend the summer with me in a borrowed duplex on Twelfth Street. The flat is through Amy's connection, an apartment owned by a filmmaker or an architect—someone I never meet.

My loose plan is to make something like Godard's *Alphaville*, but badly. I decide early on to use all of the footage I shoot. I enlist my friend Carla Mayer to be one of the voiceover narrators, along with Craig Lively, bassist and songwriter of Clint Eastwood, the best band at Brown. On screen, my friends Brendan Dolan and Chris Mitchell both play the role of the detective. I type up my script on a semibusted electric typewriter. I am nineteen.

The script has lots of gaps and typographical glitches, which Craig decides to read as if they were line breaks and rhythmic stresses. Carla sort of whines her lines, pushing the tape deck into the red, and Craig sounds like he's on Dilaudid. The plot is not exactly a plot and the detective's story is told in a Chandler-via-Bugs-Bunny-and-Groucho mash of outdated slang. I film the scenes around Brown, most of them dumb visual gags: a box of cereal disappears and reappears; Brendan plays trumpet while I play bass, our actions eventually matching the Defunkt song playing in the background.

The film allows me to splice musical excerpts end to end, throughout. I use a live recording of Peter Brötzmann and Han Bennink from a concert John Corbett presents at Brown, Zeppelin, the B-Boys, Hashim, Aswad, Liquid Liquid, ELO, and a bunch of other records. I'm proud that I loop the beat from "When the Levee Breaks" before anyone else, and by hand, like all of it, using tape. Brendan panics when we're filming in Chris's apartment and runs away, leaving me without a lead actor. One whole roll of film I shoot comes back from the lab black. None of what I shoot is beautiful.

The minute I am done with *The Take*, I know I am not going to make films. The combination of skills and personality traits needed for the work is not something I have. Jon Moritsugu is working in Providence at the same time as me and lives across the street on Hope Street during my junior year. He finishes *Mommy Mommy Where's My Brain* when I finish *The Take*, and then invites me to be in *Der Elvis*. I stand on top of an abandoned car, playing guitar and being a "rock star." I can be seen only briefly, as the film consists of hyperquick edits. Moritsugu can make the final product hum with all the energy of the moment—he's a filmmaker. It's a relief to know definitively that I am not any good at a particular thing, and that my role will be loving and studying this thing rather than trying to make it.

The Take is completed in April of 1986. Deborah, extremely supportive of my writing and the band, gives it a thumbs down when she sees it a few years later. A few other people see it and there are no raves. I am committed to being in a band, and when I return to school that fall that's exactly what happens. Bands are instant, portable, and cheap. Rehearsals are just as fun as shows. It all appeals to my impatience. You feel things instantly and get to respond to a crowd in real time. It's democratic and unpretentious.

I'm the Man (1979)

In seventh grade, Eva Lebowitz throws a party. She lives on Clinton Avenue in one of the mansion homes. The smaller homes in Fort Greene, which are still big brownstones, are apparently where the servants lived. This is what I am told but I do not verify the claim. Her parents go away and a classic birthday party is thrown. I buy Eva a copy of *I'm the Man* by Joe Jackson, probably because I want to hear it.

My friend Danny agrees with me that we should try drinking. We have not had alcohol before, other than a beer or two. I think I tried one of my dad's Schaefers before this, when my friend John Cullum came over and dared me to eat dry cat food with milk. Which we did.

Danny and O. get a bottle of gin and show up at Eva's. I have been talking to Eva on the phone almost every night. She is cheerful and gorgeous, so of course I decide that I am going to be a complete asshole and make out with her friend. That's post-facto framing—in the moment, I am terrified. I don't know how to make out with anyone or anything and I am scared that Eva and I like each other. Making out with her friend will be safer for reasons that begin making sense in seventh grade and, in the ideal arc of a life, stop making sense in adulthood.

Danny and I open the gin bottle together and are at a crossroads. How do people drink alcohol? We are familiar with juice and soda and an occasional milk. Eva has put out standard Styrofoam cups, the kind everyone used for coffee in the twentieth century. We each grab a cup and fill them to the top with gin. This is how we drink, as children, so why not stick to the plan? The gin burns wildly and floods my body with juniper weirdness. Since it is medicinal in mood, it doesn't feel unfamiliar. The buzz is intense and we stumble around, happily. Whoa! What a thing. We have another cup, exactly as big, and walk up the spiral stairs for Seven Minutes in Heaven.

As we stand together in line, I am trying to figure out what I want to do and how the system works and who will be choosing who. My body is also melting and my anxiety is both being both assuaged and magnified by the gin. What follows next is stretched out like a Charleston Chew bar, the kind we'd boost from Super Drugs and then throw away because who wants a Charleston Chew bar?

I end up in the bathroom and I cannot swear if I went in with Eva or not. It's sort of a Bill Buckner moment, in that I do something weird but don't know what it is right away. It may, actually, have not been that weird. But what happens immediately after this is that I feel newly sick. I feel unwell in a way that makes no sense to me. My body is pulling me in directions without my cooperation. Very soon, I am outside in the cold air, with Manny Howard and his father. I draw close to the car and vomit on the pavement. My only thought is "Not on the car, not on the car." Manny and his father drive me back to Carlton Avenue and I don't touch alcohol again for a year. I never drink gin again and, for an alcoholic, this is an accomplishment.

Pretty Decorating (1994)

I invite a writer to see our band play at the Knitting Factory on East Houston. Her name is Ann Marlowe and she knows Clem, our drummer. I ask her how she liked the show. She says, "You guys suck." She tells me she is starting a broadsheet zine called *Pretty Decorating*. She wants me to write for her. I ask her why she wants me to do that, since I am in a band, which is not where one finds writers. "You look like a writer," she says. She wants me to transcribe the discussion I've been having at the bar with my friend Andy Hawkins. We are mad about lo-fi cassette culture and how often authenticity is ascribed to crappy recordings. We have day jobs so we can pay for our music to be properly captured, we say. (That is a stretch you can make in a bar fight, where few will bother to point out that musicians with lots of money still choose the lo-fi option and that there are dozens of reasons to do so, not just the intentions we have recklessly ascribed to these musicians we do not know.) We believe, that night, that recording a good band poorly is as useful as introducing spelling errors into writing. I write that essay for Ann and then I write another. After a third piece, about Free Kitten (not an endorsement), Greil Marcus sends Ann a note saying that he enjoyed my writing.

How Big Is Detroit? (1993)

Deborah and I go to see Carla marry McArthur in Detroit. I've made the dance tape for the event and am excited. We arrive and end up in a strange B&B run by a family called the Schellongs. When we wake up, they give us tiny store-bought muffins and nothing else. I think of them as Republican trash, which is unfair of me. They could just be trash.

We are staying outside Detroit and also we know nothing about Detroit. As for the city and its suburbs? We have no idea where the lines are and what's what. Six years later, Ui will play the Magic Stick, but that's of no use now. Carla has given us a tidy little map, printed on a cardboard square. It's chic but it is not laid out in a way that reveals scale. The trip is, in fact, as far as a ride from Houston to 125th but I think the map represents something like the distance between Chambers and Fourteenth. Our rental car pulls in just as Carla and McArthur walk out of the church, married.

The wedding party is great fun and I dance too much. Deborah turns thirty in Detroit on this trip, which I feel even more guilty about. We miss the wedding and the B&B sucks. This is not a trip anybody wants for any birthday.

Optimism (1973)

If I have nothing to look forward to, the day goes poorly.

Bird Dog + Cheeseburgers (1980)

At some point in the spring of 1980, my mother tells me that the family is broke. I thought we'd hit the heights of humiliation in seventh grade when I was told to lie about having chicken pox for a second time. I miss the first two months of class. Apparently, it is better for me to use this easily disproved claim than to simply tell the truth, which is that my parents couldn't afford the tuition.

At this point, my mother is working at *Playboy* magazine, where she is in charge of something called "production." She arranges the physical creation of promotional items like credit-card trays and keychains and flyers. The main perks of the job are her bringing home the magazine (a wizard-level skill that cannot be dismissed) and that she seems to enjoy the work. Once, we go to a hotel for a *Playboy* event and are given a Panasonic boombox as a gift. I dream that I will get to keep it but my dad adopts it.

The place I am going to work is called Eagle Printing, in East Orange, New Jersey. It doesn't seem as if this place prints anything for *Playboy* but they are willing to do my mom a favor. I have done nothing to merit this job. There is a transit strike that summer, meaning the trip to East Orange takes roughly ninety minutes. I ride a series of buses to the Erie-Lackawanna train. The passenger cars are still very nineteenth century, with old wicker seats and iron walls painted green. The train smells like smoke and makes me feel like a character in one of the Kafka novels I am reading. I do this job for two summers, and the rides are long enough that I get through a chunk of Steinbeck, Faulkner, Dostoyevsky, and Kafka by the end of my run with Eagle Printing. I love these summers and this unbounded time.

On my first day, I ask for Phil Herman, the man who has hired me. He's not around, so the floor manager, Paul, takes care of me. He is tall and seems older than everyone and hates me. He gives me a big jug of fluorescent-green weed killer and tells me to clean up the parking lot. I go home, sob, and my mom calls Phil Herman.

The next day, I am relocated to the photo room. I have no idea how offset printing is done in 2023, but in 1980 it is done with four photo-sensitive metal plates, one for each of the CMYK colors, which are burned from black-and-white negatives. Those plates are then wrapped around the metal drums in the guts of the printing press. In the photo room, a camera that occupies most of that room creates these film sheets, roughly one and a half feet by three feet. You secure an image under glass in a rotating frame that locks into position perpendicular to a lens. In the other, pitch dark half of the room, you load the film into a door that is part of the camera, and the film is secured to the door by dozens of tiny vacuum jets pulling the film flat against the door. Then you shut it and trigger the exposure. A big stinky machine develops the film sheets, which are then sent to the strippers. "Strippers" are men working at light tables who position the negatives in light-blocking orange paper "flats" that line up with the hash marks on the plates being burned for each color. All of these are fairly expensive supplies.

I am assisting a man named Bird Dog, a one-armed Vietnam veteran. One of the strippers is also a one-armed Vietnam veteran, but is not named Bird Dog. Bird Dog does not want me to be there any more than Paul, but he has no choice. I love the job and after a week of the work, I have done a 180. At first, it feels Dickensian to have a job at the age of thirteen. (No idea if this is legal but I know from my Social Security tab that I am paid a few thousand bucks in 1980.) My friends are at camp or in that Fire Island place they talked about. Must be nice. What's nicer? Making money. My parents take a chunk for school and I keep enough to buy records and stereo equipment. I buy a new turntable that summer, though possibly nothing else.

My overall impression of not being safe leads me to realize that I can provide for myself. Whatever resentment I feel about working for my own education is subsumed by a blend of self-soothing and practicality. I like going to school and the activity is imperiled often enough that I want to work more than I want to miss out. Work's not that big a deal! These grownups at work are foul-mouthed and tall but they also aren't advanced or extraordinary. I take myself to lunch across the street at a diner that puts little aluminum bowls over the cheeseburgers as they cook. The result is larger and more gooey than any cheeseburger I know in New York. Why be in Fort Greene? I'll just have normal food and no money! Self-soothing with money is a different habit. If things are chaotic, I can just keep working and spending, a constant extrusion and vacuuming up that will distract me from other problems for years to come.

After a few weeks, everyone at Eagle seems happy enough to have me there. I am energetic and pay attention to details. I learn the machinery and work quickly. Though he's never really pleasant, Bird Dog takes a one-week vacation, which implies that he trusts me enough to do what needs doing. When things are slow, I make huge posters. There is photographic paper in the dark room that we use for proofs and other things, though nothing very important. It's probably vastly expensive to replace but I use it all the time. I make a *Sandinista!* poster, a *Scary Monsters* poster, a *Trust* poster. I am careful not to have anybody see me doing this even though it doesn't seem like I'd get into much trouble.

The one time I do get into trouble gives Paul a robust opportunity to red-card me. There is a massive tank in the strippers' room that they use to burn plates. It's another glass frame set into a metal body that exposes whatever is locked into the frame, in this case, to ultraviolet light. You slap in the plate, swing it 180 degrees in the horizontal plane so that the frame is facing down, and hit the button. The UV light burns the thin metal. You do one for each color, producing four different negatives. For some reason, I find this tantalizing and beg the guys to let me do it. Access is granted. I burn four plates, as instructed, but all with the yellow negative. Paul is furious and also thrilled to be able to yell at me. The cost of these plates is made clear. I am not allowed to burn the plates again.

I have two friends at Eagle, Mark Deloia and Bob Jones. They like music and are friendly to me. Mark is a feather-haired character, kind of *Fast Times at Ridgemont High* before the fact. Bob Jones is friendly and shorter than me. Both have mustaches. That fall, Bob goes with me to a Grateful Dead show that I do not enjoy. Bob gets me high on dirt weed but this does not help. I think the Grateful Dead will be scary and noisy because of their skull-with-lightning-bolt logo, but apparently they are not. This is apparently a very chill skeleton and everybody knows there is no such thing.

Mark is the flashier of the two. He has a car and tapes albums for me on cassette. One day, I play *Scary Monsters* in the car while we're at the car wash. I feel like a very important and cool adult, just doing the stuff you gotta do when you own a car and listen to popular music. Mark takes me to his house, where he lives with his parents. He shows me some porn magazines he has under his bed, which are more explicit than anything I've ever seen. All of the flesh is a blend of orange and pink and everybody looks ropy and weird. His phrasing sticks with me even now, delivered as he pulls out the box of magazines: "Do you still get to see stuff like this?" When was the earlier point when I would have begun seeing stuff like this? Was someone preventing me from seeing this stuff? We have some kind of dispute that I do not remember and I write FOOL on his locker with a Sharpie. He gets mad and I am reprimanded. Mark brings me into the stripping room to explain what has *gone down*. He writes out the word ASSUME and then circles ASS and U and ME.

"When you *assume* things you make an *ass* out of *you* and *me*."

The Move (1980)

After we lose 25 South Portland Avenue (owned) to bad financial management, we move into 232 Carlton (rented). The owner is a doctor who points out to me that a trespasser once tried to get in through the roof, mere feet from my room. That leads to three or four or twenty years of anxiety around noises at night. The mother of one of my best friends is murdered in her own basement around this time, and a family I know is held hostage in their home on Clermont. The roof story sticks.

The basement apartment at Carlton is being rented to a hot woman in her early twenties. She invites me in several times just to chat and be normal but I am dead terrified and never take her up on the offer. I talk to Eva Lebowitz on the ground floor for hours at a time, smelling our tenant's incense while gripping the receiver of our red push-button landline telephone.

We move to the Eagle Warehouse, located at 28 Cadman Plaza West, in 1980. Cadman Plaza West is renamed Old Fulton Street, something my father supports. He also lobbies for a plaque on the building that points out Walt Whitman edited the *Brooklyn Eagle* there. The building is easily visible from the Brooklyn Bridge, a boon when drunk in a cab. *Our apartment is right next to the Brooklyn Bridge*, and this is one of the most fantastic things about it. It feels like waking up in a child's board book every day. People also know the enormous clock on the top floor, an apartment occupied by a classmate of mine who always has drugs and throws parties and walks around very high and sad. That is, sad enough for another person in high school to notice, which is a high bar.

One reason we move is because the muggings in Fort Greene are getting less playful and a few friends are talking about guns, rather than knives, and I announce that we need to move, a reason that seems central to me but is almost certainly a distant second in relevance to the doctor selling 232 Carlton. I am almost six feet tall and sometimes carry money and will soon graduate from baby jacks to full-on stompings. We find the newly opened Eagle Warehouse apartment complex and somehow score the ground-floor apartment, the one with a big green gate and a dragon head. I'll never know how we pulled that off. We live in a triplex, mere blocks from school and most of my friends. This is an astonishing development. Over the years, my parents make it clear that this apartment is sending us into financial ruin once again. It has become tangibly and manifestly clear that things are going to fall apart at any minute because they quite obviously do. You run out of tuition money, you run out of rent, your best friends' parents cop a double shotgun suicide, your father dies. Bad things can happen and likely will.

My life at 28 Old Fulton is a dream, all things considered. I am no longer a social pariah. I am no longer a geographical outlier. Although I never have friends over, I can get to most of my friends easily. There is the High Street Station A, the Clark Street 2 and 3, the Montague Street R, and the Borough Hall rainbow of trains. Also I can get the F at York Street. It should be stressed that Dumbo, in 1980, does not exist. There is nothing there. A car service, maybe. That's it.

One day, in 1983, I make one of my many journeys into Manhattan, over the bridge to shop at Bondy's and then J&R Music World. I return with a stack of records wrapped in those yellow-and-brown paper bags and secured with packing tape. I have Madonna's debut album. I've started smoking Marlboro Lights. The windows of the building on the first few floors are fortified fortress thingies with wide deep lintels and thick mesh iron grating. You can climb all of yourself into the unusually big outdoor space between the window opening and the grate. I squinch into that space and smoke while listening to Madonna and Kid Creole and the Coconuts' *Wise Guy*. The stereo is playing but I am not technically visible, so if you opened the door, you would think me gone. This is liberation, freedom, and goodness. This will lead somewhere. I will produce these records, play bass on them, something. This music is where something is. I am light-headed with nicotine. I feel freaky and free.

Earlier (1982)

Due to an earlier incident at Forty-Second Street, A, C, and E train service has resumed with residual delays.
—Metropolitan Transportation Authority

PS122 (1993)

When Dolores is winding down in 1988, I meet a guy named Chris Wilcha. His girlfriend, Sarah Saffian, is tight with Laurel Watts, girlfriend of Alex Wright, the other bass player in Dolores. Chris is smart and good-natured and becomes a fan of Ui when we form in 1990. Alex is initially in the band until he quits to go do graduate work at the Harvard Kennedy School.

In 1992, we connect with Wilbo and fire up. In 1993, we record our first record and get rolling. Chris films lots of our shows with his portable camcorder. He arranges a show for us at P.S. 122 with Chavez, a local rock band that sound nothing like us but are great live. The show is forgettable except for when Clay Tarver asks me where he might "wee-wee."

What we remember is postering. For the first five or six years of Ui's existence, we get some great posters printed. Most of them are Jim Gallagher's monoprints, which he runs off for us. They look like blueprints, and as far as I know, are drawn on to the glass that then creates the print. Jordin Isip does a few for us, too. The PS122 poster is a four-color image created by Jim—I don't know who paid for it to be printed. It's a lovely golden color along with black—maybe it's just two-color. Ui goes out with Wilcha to poster the town. Across from P.S. 122, on First Avenue and Ninth Street, a woman approaches us. We are leaping up in the air and wheat-pasting a plywood wall.

"Who are you working for?" she asks.

"Nobody," Chris says. "We're just a band."

"Did you know this is illegal?" she says.

I'm wondering who this person is. She seems to have a microphone but I can't see a cameraman anywhere.

"No, I didn't know that," Clem deadpans, sounding completely sincere, somehow.

It turns out that Channel 9 is doing a segment on "poster sniping," which is mostly a story about the Delsner/Graham axis doing mass postering for big-venue shows. Even in those instances, it seems like a minor problem. Those firms do the work from the safety of trucks, using long poles to paste up the sheets. They don't talk to Channel 9, however. We, dumb, do. It turns out that the cameraman was in a car across the street. The segment is entertaining and we pass it around to friends in the months to come.

Fools Gold (1990)

My nineties are Deborah Holmes. We start dating on January 1, 1990, and spend almost every day together until January 6, 2006. She has an adamantine center and unerring aim. There isn't a lot of hesitation during a day with Deborah. Her wishes and thoughts are available to her and she delivers them without unnecessary bracketing. She is also, almost always, laughing.

Deborah and I bond about music from the start. She tells me about her time in the eighties going to clubs with her DJ boyfriend, Van Gosse. She has seen many of my favorite bands in tiny clubs like Trax or Tier 3: Gang of Four, Pylon, Buzzcocks. She is an ex-lawyer when I meet her, though, and sometimes her tales of mayhem and debauchery sound not exactly false but surprising, given her strong emotional sobriety and taste for early bedtimes. On our first night together—chastely snuggled on a futon—we play each other songs, like birds inflating to make our feathers catch the light. I decide to test her limits and choose Big Black's "Kerosene," a song that is more noisy than almost any other noisy guitar song, but carefully paced, with lyrics that embody a particularly American kind of self-loathing and fear. It is the national anthem of the murderous and suicidal teen: "Never anything to do in this town, live here my whole life." She loves it. She plays a song from David Byrne's *Rei Momo*, a song that twenty-two-year-old Sasha is primed to dismiss, as Byrne is now officially corny, fallen. But I feel Deborah's openness. I see her big liquid eyes and easy smile, her sweet little buck teeth, and I realize that I want to love things the way she loves them, without additional anxiety about where it might fit into the world, thinking only of where it fits inside her.

We listen to Hot 97 in the morning through her little white cube alarm clock with the segmented aquamarine numbers. I can't really overstress how good popular music is in 1990, or how ecumenical and weird Hot 97 is, a station that hovers around dance and R&B and hip-hop and pop and never makes up its mind: a perfect approach. We hear things on the radio and listen to mixtapes I make. Deborah loves all of these songs and plays them and talks about them and asks me to play them and quotes them: Black Box, "Everybody Everybody"; Poor Righteous Teachers, "Rock Dis Funky Joint"; Nikki D, "Lettin' Off Steam"; Gang Starr, "Just to Get a Rep"; Depth Charge, "Depth Charge"; LL Cool J, "Jingling Baby"; Eric B. & Rakim, "Let the Rhythm Hit 'Em"; Deee-Lite, "Groove Is in the Heart"; Snap!, "The Power"; Depeche Mode, "Enjoy the Silence"; Digital Underground, "The Humpty Dance"; Sun Electric, "O'Locco"; My Bloody Valentine, "Soon"; the Stone Roses, "Fools Gold" (a DKH favorite); LL Cool J, "The Boomin' System"; George Michael, "Freedom! '90"; Sinéad O'Connor, "Nothing Compares 2 U"; EMF, "Unbelievable"; Michel'le, "No More Lies"; En Vogue, "Hold On"; Madonna, "Justify My Love"; and Chubb Rock, "Treat 'Em Right."

Hot 97 advertises a "rhythmic" blend that tends toward freestyle like Shannon and Lisa Lisa & Cult Jam much of the time while being pulled to the margins by whatever rap or dance song is rising. Manchester's rave scene is kicking in and rap is becoming top-ten music once and for all. All of the weird and marginal music I love seems to be bleeding into the mainstream. I am in love and have a set of roto-toms on the mantlepiece in the bedroom. I am starting Ui and I believe—right or wrong—that you can simply put everything you love in one place, an idea I get from Deborah.

We are not major cooks, either of us. In 1990, when we are first living together at 172 Sullivan, we walk down the block on Saturdays to a shop called Melampo, a storefront below Houston. There is a modest market selection presented on shelves on either side as you walk in, and a man behind a counter in the back: Alessandro. He makes a sandwich like he's operating on a small, scared animal. (I am told that his apprentice, Walter, runs things at Alidoro now and is almost as good.) Alessandro is offended by almost anything any customer says and likes to exile people, a trait common to New York geniuses of the nineties. Alessandro makes his sandwiches by cutting a square of focaccia horizontally, then larding it to a reasonable height with thin prosciutto, artichoke hearts, olive oil, mozzarella—there are many variations. Sandwiches are wrapped in loose, soft foil and are both warm and salty. We take them down to the tables along the basketball court a few doors down from Melampo. Deborah has sort of a crush on Alessandro and I think it's mutual, which explains how we keep avoiding expulsion. She would be heartbroken to know that people ended up calling him a "creep" in the comment section of Chowhound. Candy-asses!

When I bike in the West Village now, I sometimes think of us getting coffee and monkey bread at Taylor's in 1992 and going to sit in the churchyard at Hudson and Grove. We are doubled over, talking about people we work with at the Families and Work Institute. There is a young hire who mentions her work in Central America every fifteen minutes, earning her the honor of a tribute song written entirely in Spanish, with only one line repeated ad infinitum: "Yo estoy Linda Smith."

The famous interstitial shot of the Grove and Bedford street signs used in *Friends* is filmed from a spot in front of 2 Grove Street, our second apartment, and the first we rent together. We watch *Friends* at 392 Broadway, though—the show doesn't air until 1994 and we move into the loft during the summer of 1993. Our only charge at that point is our poodle, Deacon, whom we housebreak at 2 Grove Street. He is a romping youngster only one year old when we land on the border of Chinatown and Tribeca. We take Deacon to work with us at the Families and Work Institute at 330 Seventh Avenue, and we do this for years. He is in a cage most of the time, which he doesn't seem to mind. The nineties are different.

392 is an enormous space, big enough for my band to rehearse in, which is one of the reasons Deborah thinks we need to live there. She is always supportive of the band, and lends Ui $5,000 to make the first EP, right before we move into the loft. The space is briefly ours, for a few years. Once Sam is born, our life becomes a shifting series of sounds. We install white-noise machines outside of our room and Sam's, which is right across from our bedroom. When Jonah arrives, it occurs to us that maybe we don't need to sleep right next to two small kids. We convert the back room into two bedrooms for the boys. The band, it turns out, never rehearses back there. I worry too much that the noise will bother our downstairs neighbor Patrice, a pinched and miserable person. Instead, irony of all ironies, we have two boys, who end up bothering her more than any band ever would have.

Deborah moves steadily through her loves. There is always a book on her nightstand (a stack, actually) and in her bag. Whenever we go somewhere that involves waiting, she reads during the wait. We go to Angelika fairly often, and sometimes to Film Forum. Her interest in culture is entirely free of agenda or anxiety. We just go to the things that appeal to her, though we see very few rock shows together. She comes to every single Ui show in New York, without fail. She loves Bonnie Raitt and Randy Travis, whom I end up loving as well. I encourage her to play her tapes in the car but she says, "Well, I know my tapes. I want to hear something else."

The Last Easy Job (1994)

In 1995, Wilcha gets me a job at Columbia House, the tape and record club that has become a CD club. Wilcha is the head of marketing, or at least part of it, a young person tasked with getting Columbia House into the business of selling alternative music or whatever comes after Nirvana or, more specifically, what everything looks like in the wake of Nirvana. Late-period Columbia House is what capitalist enfeebling looks like, a bunch of not very smart people running around hoping to cram the current moment into a widget that can be sold, without understanding either the moment or the widget.

This job is ideal for a working musician. I am employed as copywriter for the catalog that goes out to Columbia House members. The whole point of the club is to lure unsuspecting consumers into usurious and moronic deals with a big loss leader—maybe ten or twenty CDs for a penny—and then lock them into passively buying CDs month after month. If they remember to say no, they won't buy that month's CD. If they forgot to check the box, the CD goes out and they pay for it. This is similar to app subscriptions, which bleed consumers for months before they remember to cancel.

We are tasked to make the catalog feel like a magazine, though not critical of the music in any way. I work in a room with the lead designer, a delightful woman named Lynda Kuznetz. Each week, I need to describe the albums being sold with or without consent to the Columbia House members. It is sales copy, tweaked to sound a bit spicy without alienating anyone, more or less the same approach of magazines and newspapers but less dishonest about the underlying purpose. The entire week's worth of work can be done in roughly three hours. There are meetings every few days in which we discuss the layout of that month's catalog, strategizing about which albums to push hardest. As this is based on what is popular on the charts and the terms of each band's (or label's) agreement with Columbia House, neither of which we can influence, it doesn't seem like this decision needs a meeting. These conversations make it feel less like we are working for the labels. (We are working for the labels.)

There are artists, though, that will not play ball with Columbia House. One of the reasons artists balk is that Columbia House makes its own product, using masters and art from the labels. They are not good at this. In the nineties, this product is CDs. In the seventies, the product was LPs, some of which were folded and put through my mail slot on Carlton Avenue. As a Columbia House member in my preteens, I drooped with disappointment when the albums arrived in the mail, months after release date, marked "CHC" on the back. Columbia House Club! A pressing nobody wants, including you.

Younger staffers mock the older managers from the seventies who are now trying to sound relevant. In a business that happily and routinely murders its elders in public, manager seems like a bad gig. Chris is able to bring his camcorder to every meeting, for reasons that are never clear. He films hundreds of hours in the office, which later becomes *The Target Shoots First*.

After Lynda is shifted to a different room, another sunny person named Marie Capozzi moves into my office. My days are spent goofing off energetically. Lynda has one of the great laughs—high and explosive with a long trail of tumbling cackles. She makes it impossible for me to focus on anything other than Making Lynda Laugh, which makes Columbia House a therapeutic and rewarding job. Our office is on Sixth Avenue, right across from the News Corp building, and all I do is lark about with sweet people, for pay. Chris and Lynda and Marie and I hang out in a small gang. Our main decisions are what to have for lunch and when to leave. The cafeteria has good curly fries but isn't fun. We don't have the time or money to eat at restaurants, though, and the options in Midtown are gruesome.

My time at Columbia House coincides with my other work becoming more involved. Ui puts out its first record in October of 1993. Sometime later, in 1994, I get a call from Doug McCombs, bassist for Tortoise. The band has heard our record and wants us to do a short tour with them and Labradford. That is fantastic news, but I don't know anyone in the band and haven't sent them our music. What happened? I had sent physical copies of *The 2-Sided EP* to a couple of labels, including Touch and Go.

Doug is working at Touch and Go and snags our twelve-inch. *Bro, what if they wanted to hear that and sign us?* But, bro, they did not. Doug has done us a mitzvah.

I am working at Columbia House when Stereolab's manager, Martin Pike, calls us. This is in 1996, about a year after the Tortoise shows. They've gotten our new single, "Match My Foot," released on a small English label called Soul Static Sound. Martin asks if we would go on a month-long tour with Stereolab. The answer is very much yes. In 1995, I start writing a column called "Bubbling Under" for the *New York Post*. The arts and culture editor is Matt Diebel, an Australian from the Murdoch empire's original HQ. The only reason I meet him is because Deborah's mother, Monika, is friends with a therapist named Arlene Kagel. Arlene is Matt's therapist.

A word on Arlene Kagel. I never actually meet Arlene and she may be wonderful. Shout-out to Arlene. But she reveals a key aspect of how Nikki (Monika's nickname) sees the world. Nikki is obsessed with status and titles and degrees and Arlene seems to have enough of these that her opinion can be adduced with authority—in fact, to the point of obviating all other arguments. She is sitting in one of Nikki's light circles and is unable to be touched. Arlene is kind enough to pass on to the Holmes family the fact that this Australian man is looking for a writer. They pass this on to me and I agree to meet him.

I go to see Matt in a bad Midtown diner near the News Corp building. He tells me that he loves George

Jones and wants to find out if people are wearing "kilts in the clubs." I tell him we are at the height of white alternative culture and the fashion sense in pop now is pretty bleak, unless I go to gay clubs or big pop shows. No, he doesn't want those—he wants the nitty-gritty clubs. He seems to want some combination of 1972 Electric Circus and 1978 Rawhide. I tell him I will do my best.

The column runs every Wednesday and gets the boldtype treatment for proper names. It's mostly about weird records and local shows and nods toward bigger acts and MCs I like. I write about Tricky's first single, "Aftermath," like every journalist in the world. Not hard to spot that one. Tricky comes to town for a gig, so I preview it for the column. Matt calls me.

"You were pretty early on Tricky, yes?"

"Not more than anyone else."

"But you wrote about his very first single, yes?"

"I sure did."

"OK, great."

As I do every Wednesday, I pick up the *New York Post* on my way to the subway. I never see proofs or readbacks. I send my copy in, we have a brief discussion, and it runs. This is tabloid stuff and I am thrilled to have some bread coming in. Columbia House doesn't present many deep challenges, and even if the *Post* column is broad strokes, it's good to have my hand in every week. Most of the time.

I pick up the paper and am surprised. My lede now reads, "Toot! Toot! That's the sound of us blowing our own horn." A writer who apparently has my name goes on to describe how ahead of the curve we were on this Tricky fella. My friends toot at me for much of the day.

When I am fired in 1996, Matt calls me while I am in some deep Columbia House–catalog tinkering—the filter over Alanis is making her look demonic and we have to pull it back—and tells me it's lights out.

"It's getting too *Village Voice*-y," he says, possibly because he knows I have been writing for them. He cites my use of the phrase "moon rocks" as evidence of figurative and vague language. Fair play! I do not regret my termination and all my memories of working for Matt are fond, except for the death threat. It was mailed to me on a Patrolmen's Benevolent Association postcard. The author made it clear he knew where I got my mail, where I lived, and what everything looked like. It was unpleasant but not Matt's fault.

Sushi with Nikki (1990)

When I meet Deborah, I am a dropout from Brown, working on Quark and PageMaker surveys for Families and Work. One of the founders, Ellen Galinsky, works originally at the Bank Street School uptown, the branch near Columbia. My friend Thalia Field puts me on to a job there, helping Ellen by typing things up. I stick with Ellen and move down to 330 Seventh Avenue, in the garment district, when she and Dana Friedman set up FWI. They provide a variety of services, including consulting to huge companies and trying to figure out how they can give executive women a break. This usually involves allowing women to make partner while working part-time, and other family-friendly moves. As Deborah herself puts it, it's advancing the cause of "white women in suits." I have nothing to do with the content of this work. I simply type up Ellen's purple-ballpoint draft pages.

Deborah has left the law to come to Families and Work. After she finished at Harvard Law, she went to work at Gibson, Dunn & Crutcher. She was sent to Alaska, to work on the Alyeska Pipeline for a company on the wrong side of the Exxon Valdez spill. It was her, a few file cabinets, and a lot of fishermen proposing marriage. She was working for the bad guys and did not like it. On a plane trip, she saw Dana Friedman on a talk show and quit to come work for her, just like that.

I see the cute lady with the big eyes in staff meetings and assume she would not be interested in a school dropout who plays in a band. Dolores is still doing shows in New York and living out its final life cycle while I plan the band that becomes Ui. We are both from privileged-asshole schools and yet somehow find the room between the bricks to lob insults at each other. She says St. Ann's isn't a real school and constantly quizzes me on state capitals because of course why would I know that, as if we just studied Bella Abzug's poems and ate communist fruit leather. (We did.) She says more or less the same shit about Brown but I deduct points for recycling material. I mock Dalton and Harvard as bastions of the corrupt and pompous, based on nothing but intramural spite. We talk, nonstop, all day, even though we only work together intermittently and she is several pay levels above me.

When I finally visit her apartment, I discover it is on Sullivan Street, right next to the childhood home of Tom Cushman, someone I haven't seen in roughly five years. I never, in fact, see him, though he pops up once in my email to ask me to give back one of the existing Brooklyn cassettes. (Brooklyn is a band he had with Adam Yauch and Darryl Jenifer.) That's my only exchange with Tom while we are neighbors in 1990.

The first time I stay over at Deborah's, I sleep on her futon. She goes out to get me a toothbrush from a bodega. We play Brian Eno's *Ambient 1: Music for Airports* and I weep about the woman I am in the process of breaking up with, Brenda Yeager. Deborah puts up with almost a solid year of me moaning on about Brenda, which is generous. That first night, we snuggle on the futon.

Deborah's mom Nikki doesn't want to meet me in any way and she hangs on to this refusal for over a year. We eventually meet over sushi after I move in with Deborah. In the course of a meal, she tells me that I am not good enough for her daughter. This is not a paraphrase—these are her exact words. She goes on to explain that Arlene

Kagel, when Deborah was four years old, determined that Deborah would be famous and successful. At this point I do not yet know who Arlene Kagel is. Institutional validation obviously plays a role in Nikki's life, and sometimes that institution is just Nikki. Deborah and I have a very awkward ride home on the A train. I am, for this moment, unsure of how to move forward. But we do.

Carrying People Around (1996)

On one tour, we are in charge of carrying a DJ around in our white van. The tour manager makes this happen, so that the headliners don't have to think about him. On our first night of playing, at Irving Plaza, the room turns orange with happiness. It is one of the three or four best shows we ever play and the headliners absolutely boil the room with their drones. As we stand outside, watching the headliners load into their bus, the tour manager comes over and tells me that we're making $125 a night (didn't know that) and the DJ is riding with us (what the).

This does not go well. The DJ doesn't like to bathe or carry his own equipment but he does like to talk. When we play Lawrence, Kansas, he tells us that William Burroughs's "people" are coming to the show. This does not transpire. In the van, after the show, after we have loaded his DJ coffin into our van on his behalf, he sits in the back seat and says, "Wait!"

"Listen to that," he says.

We have an incredibly long drive to Boulder and must start driving immediately. We are behind a film theater, in an alley, next to a bagel factory.

"Someone's bootlegged my show and is playing it. This happens all the time. They even post my setlists online before I even leave the club!"

"It's your Walkman," Wilbo points out. "You sat on it and hit play."

"Yeah, THIS TIME, but man, it never stops."

We eventually drop him off the tour so he can go compete in a DJ battle with the X-Ecutioners in Las Vegas, which sounds like suicide.

The Men and Women of Tax (2008)

I rate the men and women of tax.

To satisfy an IRS audit, I print out every transaction with my bank. This is more pages than things normally are. By my fifth visit to the IRS branch on Forty-Fourth Street, I feel warmly toward the tax agent named Richard. He tells me that my file has "kicked out" because it is a Schedule C. Lawyers and doctors and other self-employed people file Schedule Cs and have no compunction about claiming a huge chunk of their income, illegally. That I have not done this and am also not a doctor or lawyer has no bearing. My file kicked out. This is the ontology of the IRS. Once a thing has happened and is in the system, it is sanctified.

I am a contracted freelancer for the *New Yorker*, and I work forty hours a week in an office. I am not given health benefits by my employer, which someone tells me is illegal, given the hours and the office. In a moment of idiot optimism, I think this is what has triggered the Feds, like they might roll up and say good day sir what is all this money for doctors come on this is no way to live lol.

Richard eventually tells me there is nothing wrong. The IRS just didn't know what to do with a bank transfer between me and my ex-wife. I explain that we have kids and he says cool ok no more audit you can take your 825 pages with you.

That's the Feds. New York State is savage but good on the phone. The California tax board can eat dirt.

Just a Dream (1986)

I'm living on East Eleventh Street with Amy in a two-story apartment that some photographer has lent her. She is working as a PA on a film called *Skip Tracer*. I don't know why this adult has done this generous thing. For a summer, we live in his eighties: glass brick, spiral staircase, shower with good water pressure. The video for "Walk This Way" is on MTV several times a day. We order in or go out. I am lucky to be where I am.

The only bands I see twice in 1986 are Sonic Youth and Trouble Funk. As much as I love rap, it only feels coherent on my Walkman or on the dancefloor. In a club, the DJs and dancers create a living network that feels like a performance. Live rap shows, though, are terrible, without exception, because the acts are not doing what they did in the studio. Some develop skills for both modes, but not many. It does not make any sense to think of rap as a way for me to make music. I want to be in the Compass Point All Stars or the S.O.S. Band, which is not going to happen, so I have to find a way to play a kind of music that has room for me to make what I'm hearing.

In July, I see a Sunday-night show at CBGBs: the Homestead Records showcase, which has been appended to the New Music Seminar. The bill is Great Plains—whom I do not see—Live Skull, Volcano Suns, and Big Black. Live Skull are chilly and energizing; James Lo has a way of playing roto-toms that I've never seen before or since, sounding like a hail of plastic buckets hitting the floor. Volcano Suns are a benevolent mess, more like their name than any other band of that time. Steve Albini begins the Big Black set by screaming, "Clear out! Clear out! You didn't pay!" which is true of many journalists standing around me. I, however, have paid, and do not clear out. I love this band and it is my first time seeing them. They sound ferocious and grouchy but loose, and I miss the precision, a pleasurable fetish focus on the records. After a few songs, their Roland drum machine stops working. Peter Prescott of Volcano Suns sets up his drum set and plays along for "Kerosene." Not bad but also not the catharsis through detail that I wanted.

Two weeks later, Sonic Youth play CBGBs and they play many of the songs from *EVOL*. Kim Gordon drops down into a whisper for "Shadow of a Doubt." My tiny brain rumbles into popcorn and wafts away. I've been going to hard-music shows for years now. I'm not a hard-core guy, as much as I love Bad Brains. I love Big Black but I don't want to sing about babies being raped. Sonic Youth have arrived at a space in my head.

"Shadow of a Doubt" is mostly harmonics for the first minute. It's as intense as any of the loud numbers without being particularly noisy. It isn't even exactly rock. This is that part of the eighties when something cracks and all of this misshapen orphan music flows out of New York like lava, all the bands that didn't want to play barre-chord *bash bash bash*. (Liquid Liquid and DNA are part of this seven-year pitch.) Everything is wide and light and unnamed. Kim Gordon makes it seem like anyone might be in a band. Sonic Youth look more like the *Peanuts* gang than any of the other groovy ghoulies. (Butthole Surfers want to be terrifying and they are.) Sonic Youth aren't working very hard to seem insane, an act of massive importance in 1986 to a lot of independent rock bands. They go for shock, sometimes—they do the Manson references and bad-slasher-movie makeup in one video. But they don't sell the psyche of horror, just the fandom, and even that works only at a distance. In person, they burn warm. The crowd sways along with "Shadow of a Doubt" and my consciousness toggles. This music is neither violent nor nonviolent and we're in the ocean with them. Nobody moshes or thrashes or slams.

Over the course of the set, they sound like staplers and play Madonna through a boombox and fuck up a bunch of times and don't make a big deal out of it. I'm not thinking about my place in anything when I walk in. I just want to hear these bands, and my own work is just a problem in my pocket. This song changes that. I need this to happen to me in a systematic way. At the end of the summer, Amy leaves me for my friend, Tom. I go back to Brown and start Dolores.

Six Day War (2002)

I haven't been in many bands that play normal rock music, not because of some Firm Belief. Not that many people ask and I don't write many rock songs like that. But in the early 2000s, I get to know the guitarist and writer Alan Licht through Tim Barnes, a drummer and connector and beautiful person. Barnes works at a place called Lost Planet that does music-sync licenses and post-production. Tim helps me get the biggest paycheck I've gotten from music: $30,000. I make a solo guitar record for Sub Rosa in 1998 called *Standing Upright on a Curve*. (More accurately: half an album. The second half is work by Loren Mazzacane Connors). I write those pieces for my father, after his unexpected death in 1997 and the very expected birth of our son, Sam. I record most of the tracks in Sam's nursery when he isn't sleeping in it. Tim sells a track called "Steep" to a cable company in California called Media One or Dominion One or Something One. I own both the publishing and writing for that track, so I am able to get two checks. Tim introduces me to Alan, who is putting together Six Day War, a rock band designed (loosely) to play the poppier songs he's written over the years. Tim plays drums, I play bass, Dean Roberts sings (sometimes), and Alan sings and plays guitar. Alan has done straight song material in Love Child but also makes nontraditional and experimental guitar music. Is that the right way to describe it?

I love being in this band and want to do more. We play one live show, at Maxwell's. As part of this set, we cover Bad Brains' "Banned in DC" and Dean goes appropriately nuts "as H.R."

Beverly Boys Club (1976)

I want to play baseball in 1976. I see little league teams on TV and in movies, and they seem as real as those Dairy

Queens a friend of mine went to in Philadelphia. But, in the seventies, New York is the hot location for people opting out of Mass American Behavior. No chain stores, no big American sports, no niche fast food. We are all burning buildings and opera and newspapers and block parties and basketball. If you fall in love with a piece of common America, you're out of luck.

In third grade, a new kid named Russell Moorman comes to St. Ann's. It is the last year of being grouped into all-day classrooms. The next year, in fourth grade, we'll have Trapper Keepers and lockers and roam around the upper floors from 4 all the way up to 12. But in third grade, we still work and play as a self-contained pack. That year, I play Caiaphas in *Jesus Christ Superstar*, bare-chested with my mom's woolen cape for a costume. Russell is one of the few Black kids in the school and he doesn't seem to bond to anyone, not right away.

One of our daily tasks is to practice writing cursive in a thin composition pamphlet. Each one has pale blue covers and big, loose pages ruled with dotted lines. Russell writes quickly in phenomenally neat script. Those who finish are allowed to play in one of the sandboxes in the anteroom. Nobody ever finishes before Russell and he always chooses the dry sandbox, which seems less fun than the wet. It takes me a while to recognize that he chooses this box precisely because nobody else is going to bother him there.

I work up the courage to talk to Russell one day, in the lobby. He mentions that he plays on a little league team and I lose my tiny mind. St. Ann's has basketball teams and some sort of ragtag soccer team but no equipment and no field. We simply play what we can in Cadman Plaza Park, which is mostly dodgeball, touch football, and a bunch of running. Almost entirely on my own, using checks my parents agreed to write, I get myself enrolled in the Beverly Boys Club. I have to take the train into Flatbush, a neighborhood I have no familiarity with. I go unaccompanied, every time, possibly because my parents don't offer to help. Which is fine. Except for the one day I get lost and somehow find Russell's house. His mother feeds me McDonald's while I cry and suggests a route to the ballfield.

I am afraid I will be mocked for being named Sasha, so I use my legal name, Alexander, which a coach shortens to "Alec." The next year, it is adjusted to "Alex" on my trophies. Some of them are participation prizes for being on the Jet Stars, but twice I win a Golden Glove for my work at first base. I am a miserable batter but I love fielding. That split second between release and catch allows me to position myself and lean into the ball. Batting doesn't give me that extra decimal point. I get hit by a pitch once, which seems way beyond any kind of reasonable risk. That simply isn't going to happen in basketball, which I cannot play.

Kate Brodsky (1978)

The first girl I ever pass a note to is Kate Brodsky. For some reason, St. Ann's sends some middle schoolers on a trip to the beach. Several of us hunch over a deep hole in the sand that we dig as an excuse to not look at each other and talk about deep things. It emerges, in a public way, that I think Kate Brodsky is cute, intel I cannot contradict. The plan is to slip her a note, which I do, though I can't remember what it said. The folded paper is delivered and she comes back with a positive reply. I remember nothing about what we wrote to each other. I remember looking over a dune and feeling a kind of surprise and elation, like something forbidden has happened but not in the wrong way. A rule has been revealed as unjust and I have seen what a life in the light might be.

Years later, Kate and I end up going to Brown. She is one year behind me and a wizard in squash, one of the few sports that seems important to people in my seventies. There is a lot of squash played at the Heights Casino on Montague, though all I can afford to do there is play *Space Invaders*. This does not feel like being kept out of a fancy club or being Cinderella or some such thing. Squash looks fun but no better or worse than stoop ball. At Brown, Kate and her team go to Montana's on Thayer to celebrate after a big match. Not knowing the chili contains peanut butter, Kate eats it, goes into anaphylactic shock, and dies. Her family members became big crusaders for nut-allergy awareness, and it seems their work has been successful. Kate seemed like a pure and benign person and this story has always made me irrationally angry at all the restaurants on Thayer Street, not just Montana's. Any time I come to Providence to play a show, I glare at all the storefronts.

Ouija (1980)

I go to a sleepover at a friend's house. We are teenagers gorging ourselves on bravado. We do a Ouija-board session and I confess that I have a dream where Rachel Griffin kisses me and has electric lips. That week is heavy on the "electric" teasing, and variations on kissy lips. I think, "Bro what a dream. How can you be mad?"

Rubber Cement and Halloween (1979)

It is becoming increasingly clear, as the seventies come to a close, that something is wrong with the whole funding vibe in my family. We don't have money for nice sneakers or vacations or really anything beyond my brother and me going to a fancy school and eating.

For this Halloween, I want to be Mr. Spock. For a few years, I am passionate about *Star Trek*. This comes and goes like baseball but is just as intense while it lasts. We cannot afford any official costumes and, in the late seventies, there really aren't any. If there had been an official Star Trek™ jersey, it would have been $100 or something. Instead, I wear a blue turtleneck I already own and my mother cuts out a little silver chevron to serve as a Starfleet badge. I think the silver color is pencil, rather than silver wrapping paper or mylar. I note that.

The rest of my costume is where, shall we say, the rubber meets the road. Spock is distinguished as Vulcan (half-Vulcan, as we all know) by his pointy ears. (His haircut could be his human half.) To mimic this bodily attribute, my mother pinches the tops of my ears together and joins them to themselves with rubber cement. My alarm is immediately practical. I worry not that this will hurt but that it will not hold. My mother assures me, against reason, that this will work. We pull a beanie over my head and away I get on the B38.

I spend the day in class with this dumb hat on. Everyone wants to know what is under the hat. Nothing, of course, why do you ask. Eat your Tiger's Milk bar. After school, while playing touch football in Cadman Plaza Park, one of my friends rips the beanie from my head. There is, of course, nothing to see. I am now, all of a sudden, explaining the extremely shady-sounding idea that my mother rubber-cemented my ears into a Vulcan peak, which makes it sound like I am accusing my mother of child abuse. I am embarrassed for her: I know the rubber cement idea is impractical and motivated partly by a desire to please me but also very clearly (it seems) by a desire to achieve plausible deniability—"Well, I tried!"—while leaving me with the burden of explaining her insane idea to my friends. I am mad she didn't just tell the truth and say, "We're broke for no good reason, so you can't be Spock."

Nobody believes me. I opt out of trick-or-treating.

Elvis Dies in DC (1977)

In August of 1977, my brother and I are sent to live with some people we barely know in Washington, DC. This is because my family does not yet have a permanent home. We go through the blackout with the Wingate family, on Clermont, and we move into 232 Carlton for the winter, but we have one last gap, and this is my parents' Hail Mary. Go—go there.

This family, whose name I forget, lives across the street from us briefly on South Portland. They have some children but as far as I know, neither my brother Tobias nor I really know or like anybody in the family. Nevertheless, there we are at the peak of summer, in Washington, DC. Though I do not know a single one of their names, I remember three things clearly.

It is a suburban sort of house with pale carpeting. One day, to amuse us or maybe satisfy a request we've put in, they take us to see Washington Stuff—the Smithsonian, the monument, other buildings of historical note and general importance. Every place we go to is white-and-pale-gray marble and concrete, a big sun bowl that reflects the brutal rays back onto us. We bring no drinks and this family does not allow us to venture off and buy any. The point is to see every sight in one unbroken chain and then leave.

I steal a cap pistol and firing caps from one of the kids and maybe also a big bag of change. I get away with stealing the change.

The lowermost floor is where the bedrooms are, along with a sunken living area. On August 16, I walk downstairs and one of the cracker-barrel parents is all sad and shit. Elvis Presley has died, maybe on the toilet. I don't know who he is. I am sad because I think the Fonz and Elvis are the same, and I like the Fonz.

The Psychopharmacologist (2011)

The psychopharmacologist recenters herself on the physioball. "You are mildly dysphoric. It's right here." She points to a folder I can't see. Apparently, two years ago, she figured it all out and wrote it down. Since then, we've been meeting to renew a Xanax prescription first issued in 2005. The drug provides temporary calm and endless attachment. It does nothing to stop my brain from screwing into itself.

I ask the doctor if I'm depressed. I ask her about variants of anxiety. I tell her about theories I've run across. I ask if I'm bipolar.

The psychopharmacologist is in her late fifties, glows more than people glow, talks about weightlifting, and shows me underwater photos she took while snorkeling with her husband, someone joined with her in the fight against senescence. My brain and its measure are just part of her achievement matrix. When the doctor reminds me what she wrote down, the point is not that I've been diagnosed and will be treated, but that it is pointless for me to think about my broken thoughts when a doctor has already determined my condition. I listen to another story about the flowers of Papua New Guinea, leave with my prescription, and never return.

Moving to Florida (1985)

I listen to lots of records with John Corbett. He has a clear-vinyl copy of *Cream Corn from the Socket of Davis* by Butthole Surfers and a very nice Denon turntable, more like office gear than furniture. The unbuckled and crunchy and spittled nature of the music makes me bananas. I want to be in a band that feels this alive and tactile and mysterious and fucked up. Corbett plays me lots of records on labels like FMP and Black Saint, jazz and improvisation that just staples me to the texture of fingers and the pulse of legs, all the tumbling physicality and collective independence made true and eternal.

Block Drugs (2017)

We are a sprawl of infirmity here at Block Drugs. A woman at the counter is not buying anything. She is dropping jam jars and picking them up and looking for cracks. A man is leaning across the pharmacy counter and pushing the Chiclets so deep into the display that they spill out over the sides and hit the floor like rain. A man is sitting down and trying to arrange three packs of underwear that he can't hold.

Burt Lancaster vs. Rodan (1979)

My father and I watch movies together, all the time. His taste in movies is reliable. We do not disagree. On Saturday mornings, we watch science fiction movies like *Them* and *The Day the Earth Stood Still* and all of the movies in the *Godzilla*-family franchise. Whenever Channel 9 is showing something good, he tells me. One night, he drags me downstairs to watch *Sweet Smell of Success*. It is on at 9 p.m., which seems extremely late at the time. We see plenty of movies in theaters, though not as many as other families. The *Star Wars* premiere is a highlight: first show of the day at Astor Plaza cinema on Forty-Eighth Street. Pure joy.

Three years later, we see a Saturday-morning showing of *Alien* in Times Square. The idea is that the crowds will be smaller and they are. This movie is not like *Star Wars* or *Close Encounters*. It's beautiful and haunted and nasty. The chestburster scene with John Hurt is not a category of thing I've ever seen in a movie theater. I have popcorn and the theater is freezing cold and by the end of the movie I am so scared that my teeth are chattering, which is something I've seen depicted in cartoons but never thought was derived from reality any more than stretching necks and popping eyeballs are. But there I am, chattering, unable to detach from Ripley and her emotional journey around this monster.

Look Sharp (1982)

My godfather, Uncle John, who was my father's lover in college, comes into money and starts buying me lavish presents for my birthday. While the money is there, the gifts are really notable and important. He buys me my small Marlboro amp, a fifteen-amp buddy that is still the best amplifier I've ever owned. He buys me the puke-yellow MXR distortion pedal, also unbeatable. Then, one year, I go a little sideways and ask him to take me to Patricia Field and some shops on St. Mark's, like Trash and Vaudeville. The shopping spree feels like shoplifting in the sense that it feels wrong and demented in the moment. We buy a black satiny spandex jacket crisscrossed with zippers and pointy white boots, very much like boots on the cover of Joe Jackson's *Look Sharp!*, and green wraparound sunglasses. Why do I think I can pull this off? I am way too babyish for any of it. I wear the boots to school once. Nobody mocks me but it is not the way forward for me. I will always gravitate toward outlandishly dressed people though.

Driving with Myrna (1986)

Myrna picks me up at WBRU in her car. We drive into a forest and around a pond, talking until dawn. This isn't preceded by a date or followed by a date and the drive itself is probably not a date. The car is something like a Ferrari or a DeLorean or a Lamborghini, things I've never seen.

The Clash at Bonds (1981)

When I am fourteen, I see the Clash. They're playing for two weeks at Bonds, a shirt store in Times Square converted into a club. I cut school and stand in line all day on a Friday with Tom Cushman and Jess Siegler. I have never stood in line for so long and after that I only do it once more, sleeping out for U2 tickets during freshman year of college. This seems untrue but it is true.

When we get to the ticket booth at Bonds, we have the option of buying tickets for the first night or the last night. Which will be more historic? I opt for the first night and my friends choose both. On May 28, we all go to Bonds. My excitement is somewhere to the left of religious and sexual. I cannot believe I am about to pass into the land of the people who have seen the Clash. The club, which is just a massive white space, is insanely crowded. Like, really fucking crowded. We secure a spot in the middle, toward the front. We will not be moving.

Several local bands play and I am getting thirsty and dizzy. I know Grandmaster Flash and the Furious Five are going to play but I don't know when they are slated to start. To make a point, Joe Strummer has announced that the Clash will be showcasing local bands during this whole stand. That's nice of him.

The Furious Five finally take the stage. Thank god. They are wearing lots of leather and fringe and tassels. They are kinda Village People and the Temptations combined and revived on the cheap.

The crowd does not like this rap band. The N-word flies. I am not sure what is going on. This is unexpected but not in the way I expected to encounter the unexpected.

New York? We are doing this? O Hell No. The band gives up and leaves. Joe Strummer comes out and says big mad things. Now we have to wait longer. O Hell No 2: The Return.

I am physically and morally defeated but will not sacrifice my real estate. I hang on, several feet away from my friends. We have drifted slowly apart, crumbs in a fluid of bodies. The Clash emerge, looking dour and cool in every aspect. How does one be this cool? How did they figure out this balance of caring and not caring? They play "Clampdown" and it sounds good but not coherent. Someone is playing off the beat and everything sounds thin. I expected thunder and I'm getting rumbles. My body is about to bail on me, so I relinquish my spot and go to the bar. I cannot believe how many people are jammed into this space.

The bartender gives me a Coke with no hassles. It is the greatest beverage I've ever had up to that point, and is probably still top ten. I've seen the Clash but it's unclear if this is a good or a bad thing. It emerges the next day that Bonds has oversold the venue by some huge factor. The fire marshal closes the club after I leave the concert that night. There is all sorts of public argy-bargy and the whole run of shows is rescheduled. It sounds like the other shows are a great deal of fun but I would not know about that.

Gulp! (1977)

My dad stashes porn from the 1950s in the back of a file cabinet drawer. A standard leather photo album holds a hundred or so black-and-white photographs of what seem to be sailors and prostitutes, or people playing those roles convincingly. The men are in much better shape than the women, which is something I should have paid attention to. I become very fond of all the women and their bob haircuts. In high school, this small package begins to include full-color magazines of young hairless men having sex with each other. This is not the first evidence of my dad's sexuality. Before I know anything about his former relationship with my Uncle John, I find out that he has cowritten the lyrics for a "gay musical farce" called *Gulp!* It is 1977 and I am ten, so these data are just opaque the first time around.

The Lovin' Oven (1975)

My parents are professionals, doing jobs that mean little to me. My dad writes ad copy. "Copy" seems to be "words." Sometimes, he works for companies I recognize. *American Heritage* magazine is a thing I've maybe seen in a doctor's office. Mostly he works for acronyms: BBD, M&O.

At some point, we start an in-house bakery called "The Lovin' Oven," which produces homemade soaps and bread. For a moment, this is my mother's job or maybe our job. My brother and I mold shaved Ivory bars into balls and douse them with fragrances and oil. A ball is a good shape for soap. I have no hand in the bread production. The labels on our products are pink and have been professionally printed, because getting things printed for other people is my mother's job. Or was and will be again.

Twelve-Inch Singles (1983)

I pay attention to twelve-inch singles. They're big and have instrumentals and dub versions on the B-side. It is not as if I don't understand that the vocal A-side is the focus, the bit that goes on the radio, but then again, both sides are the same size and if something has been printed on this fancy vinyl record, it must be important. I usually find the B-sides more compelling, because very few bands have a singer like Billie Holiday or Otis Redding, so subtracting the vocals is rarely a loss I feel. I love Thomas Dolby but I'm not that attached to his voice. The dub of "Dissidents" is so compelling, little urgent scraps of singing with all this bass cracking and typewriter metal. It's more than enough—it's better. I pick up the bass guitar because it is central to all the acts I like in 1983: Minutemen, Gwen Guthrie, Duran Duran, James Blood Ulmer, Davy DMX, Grace Jones, Killing Joke, David Bowie, the Jazzy Five,

Spandau Ballet. The bass player becomes an auxiliary player, at best, by the next century, but for the moment it's the heart of the game.

St. Tropez (2010)

What is wrong with rich people?

VIP Shit (2009)

The event is paid for by a vodka company. The focus seems to be an R&B singer. I sit in a VIP section a few feet above a small dance floor and stage. The room is not suited to be a venue. I am in the West Twenties and all of a sudden aware of how dumb my job is, how truly unimportant. There is plenty of free vodka and I am still an active alcoholic, so I go to town. Atypically, though, I stop drinking early and float. I am hoping, somehow, to find something to write about.

All of a sudden, I am sitting next to Ice-T and Coco. Of course they're here. We strike up a conversation. Ice-T says he doesn't want to talk on the record, which seems fair. I mention that my older son likes him.

"Oh, from the TV?"

"No, the records," I respond.

"Off the rhymes! He likes the rhymes! Man, that makes my day," he says, seeming genuinely surprised and happy. I assume nothing better will happen so I leave and go straight home, which is also atypical.

Years later, I am in a trailer with Timbaland, Chris Cornell, and both of their wives (who are also their managers). This is not how interviews usually go. Timbaland has produced a Chris Cornell album called *Scream* but nobody will play it for me, even though I have flown to Miami to hear the album called *Scream*. We are on the set of a commercial that Spike Lee is directing. He is chewing out an underling.

"I teach film school! You wouldn't have a job! Don't tell me anything!"

The awfulness outside matches the awkwardness in the trailer. It seems that the main task here is to prevent me from learning anything. The wifeagers answer some of the questions, which is also not kosher. When I ask who plays what on the album, Tim says that he and Chris played and wrote everything. This seems completely implausible. I get nowhere, so I leave the trailer and call the *New Yorker*. I can't find my editor so another trusted party, Daniel Zalewski, talks to me. He encourages me to hang in.

Eventually, I am allowed to drive myself to Tim's house nearby. It's a massive mansion-esque house. He plays me half the album in his home movie theater and tells me it's his "masterpiece." It sounds chaotic and genuinely unformed, like music from no particular place. When *Scream*, the album, finally comes out, after many delays, it emerges that there are nearly a dozen different songwriters and musicians on the album. It tanks so badly that Cornell immediately returns to Soundgarden and starts touring.

Prince and the Palladium (2014)

In March of 2014, I get an email from an editor at *Essence* magazine. She asks me if I can write a cover story, the subject of which can only be revealed by phone. I call, and discover that the artist in question is Prince. I ask if the editor knows I'm white and we laugh like easy-breezy buds. Though *Essence* is targeted at Black women, they are OK with using me for this piece. The magazine apparently gave Prince a list of three writers—me, Questlove, and someone else—and he chose me.

This isn't my first contact with Prince. In 2007, I see him play Las Vegas and write about it for the *New Yorker*. He is the artist whose work grows up with me and tracks me. If there is a limit on human musicality, I assume that Prince represents that limit. It is not accurate to say I love him; it is more accurate to say I learn from him and accept what he does as an ideal. The Las Vegas show is pretty great. His new band, Third Eye Girl, is showy and muscular; the highlight is his acoustic interlude, performed on a stool with guitar. "Raspberry Beret" is when I feel the liquid mercury, or something equally treacherous and cold, entering my bones. It is not that his performance is unpleasant, but that it is so complete I will be at some grave and essential disadvantage when the moment is over.

A year after the *New Yorker* piece comes out, *Essence* informs me that Prince wants me to write something on the walls of Paisley Park. This does not make sense. Prince's reputation as a cruel prankster suggests that I steel myself.

Am I writing homilies for him? Praise? Will this be like the writing that wraps around the US Treasury? Am I writing in a specific meter? After many vague emails, it emerges that Prince is coming to New York and a man named Raul will be in touch. A date is made for 9:00 p.m. at an as-of-yet undisclosed location in Manhattan. I am to await further word. The date arrives, and Raul starts sending me word roughly every hour, starting around seven. Prince is having one dinner, first, then maybe another, and will maybe then meet me. This goes on until 1:00 a.m., when I tell Raul that I am going to bed. I hear no more from the Paisley People.

The editors at *Essence* are well aware of Prince's tendency to punish those who approach him and they are supportive. There is a small agreement I must sign with the Paisleys, guaranteeing them that I will wait as long as necessary and will not complain about Prince's approach to chronological time. I will not drink or smoke around Prince or curse. I cannot record our conversation but I can bring a pencil. This is more or less what I expect, as his methods have been widely reported. No surprises yet. I will attend a show at the Hollywood Palladium by one of his protégés, a singer named Liv Warfield. After the show, between 10:00 p.m. and dawn, I will get some time with Prince. The meeting will go on as long as he deems appropriate and no longer. To quote Elliott Gould's Marlowe, "It's OK with me." *Essence* knows there may be mischief and pays half of my fee upfront.

I arrive early at the Palladium and wait nervously until eight, when the house opens. There is a ticket waiting for me, which is a relief. I find that I am seated in the balcony, very far stage left, almost parallel with the proscenium. At best, I can see what is happening on the far edge of the stage. If I crane, I can see a sliver of downstage. Something I've heard about Prince rises like bile, the story of him inviting someone to dinner but never seating or feeding them. Why in the world would he give me a seat with no sightlines? The show is not sold out but I'm not about to steal someone else's seat. There is nobody else in the balcony. It feels like someone is watching me. Prince apparently always has people monitoring the people he interacts with. I email *Essence* asking if I can get a plus one. I want someone to sit with me in Siberia until I can finally see Prince. Prince's tour manager denies my request.

I go downstairs, buy an overpriced whiskey neat and post a selfie to Instagram. I am jittery and it seems right to send a picture of myself out into the world, an alchemized distress signal. In the caption, I make fun of myself for being a journalist "playing to rules." I down my dram and traipse up and down the velvet-carpeted staircases. I like the faded theater-elegance vibe. I have at least four, maybe six hours to go. I walk upstairs to my seat, even though I know there is nothing to watch. The opening act hasn't started. I figure I can have one more drink before our meeting. I buy a beer from the sole mezzanine salesperson and find a seat. I don't know how to prepare. I have not worn purple and am not planning to be clever, as he allegedly hates both.

All of a sudden, two men lift me up. One of them cuts off my wristband. They are not talking. My phone erupts—it is *Essence* on the line. His people, as expected, have been spying and allege that I am "drunk." I must leave the premises. The piece is now in jeopardy and if it happens at all, it won't be with me. I am suddenly outside.

I'll never know why Prince did that and I'll never know if I was "drunk" or "someone who had two drinks" and if any of it matters. I imagine Prince had this humiliation in first position and would have played his hand regardless. To their credit, the editors at *Essence* are understanding.

A Summer of Listening (2019)

The most popular song on Unit B3 is "I'm Blessed," by Charlie Wilson. By popular, I mean that more than two patients ask for it. On Sundays, Diana takes requests and connects her phone to a Bluetooth speaker that looks like a tube of cookie dough. If a song is on YouTube, Diana can play it for us. She doesn't have a long history with "I'm Blessed." A week before I get to the psych ward, Josie tells her about the song. There is a white canvas bag hanging from the front bar of her walker, on which she has written "Josie's Cadillac Escalade" with a Sharpie she isn't allowed to have. Josie calls herself "Jojo Dancer" but nobody else does. Several times a day, she tells us about her next outing. She is planning drinks at Molino's and a night at the Radisson, maybe after a trip to Target. Josie says, "Are you ready to experience White Plains and New Rochelle?"

She wants everybody in the ward to hear her. She is convinced that she is being ignored, which is true. But Josie is more up to date on Charlie Wilson than I am, which gives me one of many opportunities to not underestimate the people around me.

"I'm Blessed" could be the theme song for a cartoon cheetah who lives in a field of sunflowers. It's from the school of pure positivity that also claims Pharrell's "Happy," a song I cannot abide. It's just 1 = 1 = 1. I don't generally like music that does what it advertises. If it's a party song, it has to be demented, like Black Uhuru's

"Party Next Door." Michael Rose sings with dread, so much of it that next door sounds like the last place you want to be.

I want to hear "I'm Blessed" because I realize I am blessed. I didn't want to hear "I'm Blessed" because I didn't want to admit I needed something so simple and that I liked a song for the most obvious reason. But here I am agreeing with it. "Waking up, thanking God, every day is feeling just like Sunday." I am not thanking God but I am thankful. I have Medicaid, I am alive, I like powdered eggs.

I also might like the song because it is the only one Diana plays that I haven't heard before. I cannot find a new relationship to "Lean On Me." Diana is singing the words loud and tunelessly. Michael, the one who wants to die and refuses to eat, is sitting up straight and not exactly smiling but almost smiling.

Charlie Wilson used to be the lead singer of the Gap Band, a band I loved in high school and love now, perhaps more than before. The Gap Band did nothing exactly like anyone else. The 1982 single "Outstanding" is a slow song that is too syncopated and alive to feel really slow. It is both casual and hot-wired, in part because of Charlie Wilson's feverish dedication to changing his delivery depending on the line. If you listen to the piano do a little kick step, and then ooch up the patio steps, you'll hear the exact moment when it's time to spin on your heel. It's a popular song that is maybe only R&B because three Black brothers from Oklahoma performed it. You could turn it upside down, shake out the screws, play it on acoustic guitar, and it would belong in any genre.

Until I was a client on Unit B3, I hadn't given credit for the Gap Band's elasticity to Charlie Wilson. I hadn't paid attention to how much he was doing. There aren't many careers like Charlie's and the closest parallel is Björk, except the Gap Band are much better than the Sugarcubes. You can see two discrete, tangible careers chained together. Charlie Wilson has spent the twenty-first century being a gospel and R&B performer while filling in the spots that used to be occupied by Nate Dogg and Warren G. He is the guy that sings real good on Snoop and Kanye and Tyler tracks.

"I'm Blessed" is only gospel in subject matter. Wilson sings light and keeps the song organized. It wins me over because it doesn't plead its case, and this tricks me into being clear with myself that I want what the song has. Wilson is blessed but isn't asking you to be blessed or pushing God. "Ask me how I'm doing, I'm blessed, yes." "Riding clean, living dreams, just left the barber, feeling just like Midas." I'm blessed, yes—the double rhyme and excess affirmation make it feel like Wilson is singing to himself and we're walking past him on the way to his minivan. The song never mentions a minivan but I am convinced he is always hopping out of or into a minivan.

Josie thinks the song features Snoop Dogg, who is on another album track, but not this one. Occasionally, Diana dials up the T.I. version and people end up not singing along and looking uncomfortable. We only get access to music once or twice a week, and if Diana isn't in the mood to take requests, we hear Kirk Franklin, which is pretty good.

The night before I leave B3, Josie shouts at a staffer and demands to go outside. She has already been out, along with five other people, on a short walk around the hospital. Diana has single-handedly bumped us up to level three, just so we can take this tiny trip. (I didn't know I was on any particular level until this moment.) Josie has to ride in a wheelchair for insurance reasons. We make nature-based art, gluing twigs and leaves into two round plastic frames. The art therapist's Bluetooth speaker is broadcasting a seventies playlist, which gives us Hall and Oates's "Rich Girl." I remember trying to figure out, in 1976, why Daryl Hall had an opinion about this rich girl and how they were connected. It seemed like a weird thing to write a song about.

Music in the psych ward is a relief. I drink it all in, even when it is just someone howling along to "Simple Man" (which I hate). It is not like that in rehab, several weeks later. Music is an inverted pyramid, a hollow tang, big sucky dog dirt. The boombox radio in the day room is always tuned to the local pop station. If someone moves the dial, unseen actors reset it. I can tune the radio to a new station but it is pointless. The radio always goes back to that one station. I hear "Sucker" by the Jonas Brothers so many times that it becomes an extension of the day room. Nick Jonas is a milk box to me, a banana dipped in hot sauce, a cup of decaffeinated chicory trash water, a rag dipped in hand soap. When I hear "Sucker" I am immediately someone waiting for Jell-O to be handed out while grown men argue about animal crackers.

Everybody sings along to "Old Town Road," which the DJ announces by saying, "Coming up, Billy Ray Cyrus." Poughkeepsie radio is not ready to say "Lil Nas X" out loud. Being subjected to this top ten, Gitmo-style, reveals that pop in 2019 is mostly unpushy affirmations and dopey affection, like 1958 without the sublimated libido. Nothing can offend or imply more than one thing. The rattle of borderline-seventies funk-disco is what I dream of, or music that is soggy-in-your-clothes heavy like Marvin and Sabbath.

"Bad Guy" and "Old Town Road" are the only Number Ones we have all summer and they are oblong and fantastic and nothing like each other. "Bad Guy" is all nameless sounds made with digital tools: bumpity, yaaaa, bleep, tss tss. The twelve genders rendered as two. It is intense to witness the effect on those around me. One of my friends is in her mid-thirties, experiencing her first hard nostalgia and also believing that pop's newness is still about her. She gets mad when the song comes on?

Lights out is ten thirty, which feels early when the NBA Finals are on. I get into bed around nine thirty because I don't have a roommate after the first week and that hour alone is bliss. My view of the Hudson is clear and the air conditioning unit on the floor below reassures me.

My two recurring dream characters are Richard Ashcroft and Gordon Ramsay. I dream about Ashcroft and wonder if he is OK and will get over the fact that Allen Klein robbed him of the credit and money rightfully due to him for "Bitter Sweet Symphony." I imagine Ashcroft walking around a big house in Connecticut, the kind that looks like a mental hospital. (The fact that I am in a mental hospital is irrelevant.) The building spree of the nineties, working behind that Clinton money, created rings of columned estates that looked like early twentieth-century sanitariums. I think I dream about Ashcroft because he always seems to be alone. I dream of him pacing the foyer and slowly climbing the stairs, trying to reconcile himself to the loss of his song. I think his struggle to accept an injustice is my unconscious at work but perhaps it's just because I think that Ashcroft is always trying to appear tough even though he probably doesn't feel tough all the time. When I get out of rehab, I discover that Ashcroft has gotten his song royalties back. Dreams come true.

I dream of Ramsay less often and the story is simpler. Ramsay is on vacation with people he doesn't know and isn't allowed to drink or make any of the meals. He also can't leave. When I get home, I see that he has some awful new tourist cooking show, stunt-boy crap full of othering and bluster.

When I get home from rehab, I sell my iPhone X for six hundred counterfeit dollars and summer begins. I decide to listen to one band for as long as I can. (This length of time is a week.) I choose King Crimson because I want to hear full-bleed musicality, a band playing itself to the extension of what can be done. I want music where everybody involved is filling the room to the brim. Every band probably thinks they do just that, within their idea of the possible. Maybe I just want to hear something from my teenage years, something that I've gone in and out of listening to, that might lead to my reclaiming an idea from an earlier time that I can levy against a more recently valued idea. "Whatever I think" is an area I need to dismantle. So King Crimson embodies what every day could feel like, the surface toward which I pose the question: "Do I like this? How would I even know if I liked a thing? What part of my feelings are worth paying attention to?"

I understand that the idea of "more" or "fullness" is tricky because you could plausibly argue that a band playing without any structure or predetermined plan would be the most full and most free, or you could posit that authorship itself is the problem and you need to hear music from the distant past where the performance is the only intervention between silence and sound because the text is hundreds of years old and anonymous.

I go for King Crimson because of the quality I perceive as a collective sense of responsibility, what I hear as an investment in playing a certain kind of hard in order to make King Crimson King Crimson. What I end up listening to is the album called *Red*, usually while riding a bicycle.

As I listen, I realize my choice is dishonest on at least at one level. I really never had any trouble with King Crimson's playing, all of those graph-paper hairlines and county-county figures with fingers. What I struggle with is the singing, really, and this is maybe why I go back. The singers are where the band is weakest, in the sense of being both out-of-step and vulnerable. "Fallen Angel" is allegedly about someone asking his little brother to join the Hells Angels, which doesn't work out because lil fella gets stabbed to death. This lyric drives me batshit because the scenario isn't that complicated. All of the poetic indirection is pointless. I should not have to look up a song about this!

I still love "Fallen Angel" because vocalist John Wetton is the right kind of hammy. He bleeds so you don't have to and I drink in that lack of cool. The progressive-rock nonsense works better on "Starless." As with "Fallen Angel," the lyrics were cowritten with some poetizing person named Richard Palmer-James. The words contain "ice blue silver sky," OK, and the twice-used phrase "starless and Bible black," an Anglicism for describing a night, which is fucking beautiful. The band moves with purpose through the vocal melody, long and dusty and sweet, and then they go and invent Slint in the back half. Fair play!

A friend sends me a short piece by John Berger about swimming, which contains this:

Later I swim on my back and look up at the sky through the framed glass roof. A vivid blue with white *cirrus* clouds at an altitude, I'd guess, of about 5,000 metres. (The Latin for "curl" is cirrus.) The curls slowly shift, join, separate as the clouds drift in the wind. I can measure their drift thanks to the roof frame; otherwise it would be hard to notice it.

I imagine John Berger walking through the streets of Antony, thinking about swimming and not going to the pub. His gentleness interacts with the gentleness of Masahiko Togashi, a Japanese jazz percussionist whom I discover a few weeks after I learn what a fake one-hundred-dollar bill looks like. Togashi loses the use of his legs in 1969 and keeps on drumming. My sobriety is not so sturdy that I am too good for a clear metaphor.

When Heidi and I get married on a shallow hill in Tompkins Square Park, on November 27, 2021, she uses lines from "Outstanding" (lightly edited) in her vows: "You light my fire / I feel alive / You blow my mind / I'm satisfied." I am satisfied and surprised and delighted and a little pissed I don't use them first.

Positive Digital Natives (2021)

Wave 1 of computer people seem to want only the light in the box. If they aren't hiding from view, they are at least avoiding attention. After that, Wave 2, the Myspace wave, is people who are happier in the box but willing to come out. The youngest generation, Wave 3, finds peers on the internet and also enjoys the flat world. This is somebody's dream, I think, that the internet might foster wild and unchecked interactions that also happen in the world. This cohort isn't hiding at all. They are tenants of two planes, optimists using a nihilist's tool.

Piano Lessons (1976)

When I am nine, I take piano lessons at a music school near BAM that's still there. I remember the pencil on the sheet and the German woman disciplining me, which doesn't feel like punishment. The teacher is pointing to a thing but not pointing at me. That's all. I don't resent the work. I just realize I want to do this on guitar, so I can be in a band. The bands I like don't have piano players.

Morningside (2017)

After my second night in the apartment, I wake to the smell of gardening. The sun is working through Morningside Park and the sky is high blue. The shifting disks, the rising air, the wet cake buildings, the collision of currencies, and a moneyed cohort befriending rentiers who will never believe them.

Endoscopy (2018)

You get propofol and then everyone is nice to you. If I was rich and famous I would absolutely hide in my house and have a doctor put me to sleep every night with propofol.

Nowhere Man (1987)

At the end of my junior year, I am politely asked to reconsider my options by the administration of Brown University. I have done passably as a student until the second semester of my junior year. The band I am in, Dolores, started getting gigs and I spent all of my non-band time with my girlfriend, Brenda. I didn't do much but rehearse, play shows, have sex, and sleep. The administration's position is not unreasonable.

There is some plan that summer for Brenda to come and live with me in Providence. She's two years younger and has also managed to fail out of Brown. She does not, it turns out, come to Providence but stays at home in New

York and works as a waitress. I live with my bandmate Tim Thomas on the top floor of an old wooden building on Benefit Street, two blocks away from my job making sandwiches at Geoff's. The shop was started in 1973, very tail-end late-hippie aesthetic, and is economically paired with the next-door pizza parlor, Mutt's. It's owned and run by Wyatt, the gruff sort of Big Lebowski type who does much of the hands-on work, and his business partner, Mark, a quiet Steve Jobs type who hangs out sometimes and will occasionally retrieve a soda from the Traulsen fridge when it gets busy. The schtick at Geoff's is that the staff is rude (and encouraged to be so) and that the sandwiches have funny, local names. The Cianci is named after a corrupt local politician, Buddy Cianci. The sandwiches at Geoff's are spectacular. Whatever else has happened in the intervening thirty-odd years, nothing has dimmed my memory of these meals. Many of them depend on the intervention of a steamer, a squat, beaten-up aluminum thing that has one role: you put a sandwich into a small, boxy tray and drop it into the steamer. Pull the handle, leave it for less than a minute, and the steamer has steamed your sandwich. I've never seen another shop use this tool. I suppose people fear that it will make sandwiches wet but it doesn't. All your cheese melts and the other bits get nicely warmed and a little moist, in an appealing way. The flagship item of the shop is called a Juggs: turkey, cranberry sauce, whatever fixings you want, melted white cheddar, and something called Shedd's Sauce, a lightly spiced mayo.

Even though I work there almost five days a week, I look forward to every lunch break, when I can sit in the front of the shop, look out the window, and eat a Juggs, barely twenty feet away from where I work all day. There isn't really anywhere to go and the breaks are short. Geoff's sits at the top of a hill. Down and to the left is RISD, and beyond that is the rest of downtown Providence, the business section and whatever else is there. If you leave Geoff's to go somewhere, you have to go pretty far to find a suitable base of operations.

I work there through the end of 1987 and the beginning of 1988. For most of my time there, my manager is a beautiful redhead named Jen Dollard. Jen has a thick Rhode Island accent and is merciless with every customer. During the lunch rushes, we each have to prepare up to five sandwiches at a time. Jen yells out "Egg face! Is this for here or to go?" and we all try to coordinate our steamer usage. There are lots of hand-drawn signs around the shop, several of which I've made. I'm good at fashioning graffiti-adjacent letters. I also make posters for Dolores in this way.

I work with a kid named Pete who plays drums for a local outfit called Collision Service. He is one of those people who seems like he's sixty-five when he's nineteen. Irish and resigned, he smokes on breaks and is really nice about Dolores. He's a fan and I like his band. There is daily townie/Brownie tension in the shop but not with Pete. I'm always reassured to see him in the shop. One morning, I come in crying to work and Wyatt has to have a talk with me. I wish I remember what that was about.

Wyatt lets me blow off steam by dancing around the shop like a maniac to "Nowhere Man." WBRU is on almost all the time, and when the classic-rock sequence cycles into this Beatles song, everybody clears out. I flail around the shop, all the way back to the dishwashing station, knocking things over but never too egregiously. It is contained madness and I guess the kind of thing people sometimes did in workplaces, a category of thing that does not happen now. It seems to amuse people and it amuses me although I get bruised. I tire of the routine after a while.

I work with a guy named Mark Ruisi, who talks about jerking off as a Catholic schoolboy every time we mix up certain spreads in mayonnaise jars, churning the substance onanistically with our spatulas. He has a Lucille Ball–type catchphrase, which I love: "And there it was—*gone!*"

The band is getting a sort of strange amount of work at the time, playing gigs with bands way out of our league. We open for the Screaming Blue Messiahs at the Living Room. We are booked to open for Terence Trent D'Arby at the same venue but his management throws us off the bill at the last minute, not because of what we play, but because Terence doesn't work with openers. At some point in 1987, RISD asks us to open for a new band called Pixies. God forbid you ever hear Dolores, but the drummer, Dave, and I fancy ourselves sort of hard types and imagine that we have all sorts of things in common with the more intense bands of the day, like Big Black and Live Skull and Butthole Surfers. We do not, but that's how it feels to us. We know nothing about Pixies, other than that they are on 4AD. Dave and I say, "Clan of Xymox!" in our "funny" voice and boy do we really somehow mysteriously show them. In this day before any kind of internet, there is no way to hear a new band until they actually put out a record or show up and play live. We somehow have not managed to hear this band, yet based only on the idea that they could be gauzy and fragile and not up to our levels of intensity, we decline the gig.

We go to the show, though. Watching them play the entirety of their first EP, *Come On Pilgrim*, and bits from the debut album that isn't out yet, I realize that we have inadvertently done ourselves a massive favor. We would have run through our surplus of confidence in a single night if we had opened for Pixies.

Bleeding on the Promenade (1981)

We have a Volvo station wagon, a grey sixties model with a red interior. My dad slams his finger in the door as we park on Pierpont. Bleeding, Dad walks with us down the block to the Promenade Restaurant on the corner of Montague and Henry. He puts his finger in a glass of water and it looks like a Shirley Temple.

Sign of Empire (2018)

I ride home from the Akomfrah exhibit, unsure of when Nkrumah took power. It thunders for five minutes without rain. I am standing up on my pedals and First Avenue unfurls, a banner wide and high. The kid in front of me is listening to Super Cat on a Bluetooth speaker, riding handlessly. He is holding out his arms in a Christ pose and when he hits Fifth Street, he hunkers down over the handlebars and makes a hard left into a skid. I don't know why he doesn't fall over—which is what he wants me to wonder.

When I get to Sixth, I dock the bike and walk to Seventh. A woman speaks loudly to her kids and the rain lights up when I'm twenty feet from the door. I am embarrassed that I don't know the poem called "Transfigured Night."

The Wedding (2020)

One reason people write novels is that time needs to pass for a story to sink in. It doesn't suffice to say an event is "beautiful" or that a wedding is "the most beautiful wedding ever," nor is it a case of finding that one right word, adjectival or not. It's that in a novel, there will be hundreds of pages describing the landscape and how the ex-husband helped the ailing father build the new wing, and how one mother-in-law helped the other by practicing strict British cutbacks on the branches and stems, allowing the garden to blossom, and that the bride only had four months left. And even if those pages are only marginally well written, the novelist always has time on her side. The reader has been through it, on the clock, in the way of her own time, something the novelist cannot control but can depend on. The weight of all those events and pages and time elapsed will make it all mean something more meaningful than "beautiful wedding" or "what a sad and beautiful day" or something dumb like that. Saying it all in one go doesn't take long enough and this is why novels are long or long when they are long.

The Office (1979)

My dad works at Ziff Davis, a publisher that specializes in hobbyist magazines. The titles that compel me are *Games* and *Stereo Review*, neither of which exists in the same form now. Some of *Games* is devoted to board games and video games we can't afford. *Stereo Review* contains the first record reviews I ever see. A man named Steve Simels covers what you might call the "new wave beat." They don't cover a lot of Black music. The Simels columns give me an idea of what to buy. I cut them out of the magazines and create a journal of them. There is something necessary in this unnecessary act, the cutting and the pasting, something that pleases me outside of and beyond whatever is in these clips.

Mods + Swings (1982)

We've seen *Quadrophenia* and we are mods. We wear our long trench coats and stand on the tire swings, fifteen-year-old tough guys not yet off the playground.

Room Sound (1993)

I think I know how to make a record, and yet I do not. Believing that all the other bands suck and only you know the true way is a helpful self-deception. You need escape velocity to move through the membrane of familiarity.

I like records with lots of room sound, the moments when microphones pick up the air and the shape of a space. An example of that is "When the Levee Breaks" by Led Zeppelin. John Bonham's drums are recorded in the hallway of a large mansion and sent through an echo unit. It's pretty good.

It is late at night in 1993 and we are mixing the first Ui record. It will eventually be called *The 2-Sided EP*. We have gotten a midnight-to-six slot in a good studio on Fourteenth Street. I tell our engineer that I want to hear lots of room sound and subbass on our record. This sound will be printed on vinyl, at forty-five RPM, allowing larger grooves to be stamped. More inscribed vinyl means more information, which theoretically produces higher audio fidelity. More surface area has been surrendered to the cutting needle, leaving bigger rivulets of data. On a forty-five-RPM twelve-inch disk, for instance, a passage might be rendered over two inches of space, rather than the inch and a half a thirty-three-RPM record affords.

Our engineer tells me, correctly, "All that room sound will make everything vague and it's hard to print the levels of subbass you are proposing. The needle will jump. The mastering person at the vinyl plant will just roll off lower frequencies and the mix won't sound anything like what we're hearing now." I don't listen to him because: genius. As a result, the vinyl of our first EP sounds like a band performing in a Quonset hut a block away from wherever the record is being played. The record is available only on vinyl for several years, until Southern issues it on CD and everything ends up sounding the way we intended. Sorry, guys.

Beatin' Benzos (2017)

Eight weeks off benzodiazepines, changes are most easily observed during social interactions. When I see someone, hairlines cross in front of me. Light changes quickly without rhythm.

"What is going on?"

My voice comes back to me from far away.

I try to say something else. My voice is too soft. I repeat myself. I can see the other person clearly. They are reacting, not unhappy, wondering what is wrong. I try a louder, simpler phrase. "What are you guys doing?" There are no "guys." This is just one person. It works, though. I get an answer. My car goes up on the rails. I am having a conversation and the distance between me and my own experience has narrowed. My breathing is regular.

International Bar (2019)

"Before you choke your supervisor out, stage an aneurysm."

There are no mirrors in dive bars. Nobody wants to be reminded.

Halloween in Park Slope (1977)

I don't hear anybody say the N-word until I leave Fort Greene. People must have said this word, I know, and they must have said it somewhere but they don't say it in the street. It isn't a word you hear in songs and it isn't a way to greet someone. I only know the word as a form of violence. I do not hear this word in my neighborhood. I live on the streets with my dorky yellow bike. I would have heard it.

My ideas about this word come from television. Documentaries about the civil rights era present this word as the mantra of empire, a poisonous growth neutralized by The Cleansing Waters of the Sixties. The fact that little has changed is efficiently masked by a blend of denial and decorum. The civil rights story we see on TV is that a bad patch has been gotten through, not that a bad patch has been revealed. While I'm going around believing this sunny version of history, people in Fort Greene are likely saying and thinking the word for a host of different reasons. Not outside, though, not where I can hear.

In fourth grade, I go trick-or-treating with my friend Dave and his mother in Park Slope. I arrive at his house with a canvas drawstring bag my father has brought me from the Time & Life Building. The bag is indestructible and not an item anyone else has, which makes it a good bag. It is red and lined with grey rubber. Maybe it's a way for writers to carry ice around? A way to walk around with beer? The drawstring is an inch-thick cotton strap that is not like a string. Latin words are printed in white on the canvas but I never translate them all. (*Tempus* and *vita* were "time" and "life" and that is all I know.) I am indifferent to sweets except for Reese's Peanut Butter Cups, which drive me bats. Collecting a million wrapped things on Halloween isn't as much fun as the moments when the parents try to be clever and give us fruit or books. I give away the candy I collect, which is fussy, not generous. I just hate mess.

After walking through the dusk on Fifth Street, we stop. I want to get back to Dave's house and play with his Micronauts. As we stand there talking, a kid runs by and snatches my bag.

Dave's mother raises her fist and screams "Nigger!" Aside from not being a word I want to hear anybody screaming, this is a terrible approach to getting my bag back. I am used to my things getting nabbed and those things working their way back to me after some negotiation. Nobody would have a bike in Brooklyn without this protocol. This is bullshit. My bag is gone. She has obviously said the word before. She would get voted off the island immediately.

Disco in Fort Greene (1981)

After the Beatles, and the Moog records, my first love is disco. When the "disco sucks" sentiment reaches Brooklyn, we're so deep inside the music that the mantra makes no sense.

If there had only been record stores, I am not sure if I would have found music. The specter of the evil record store clerk presages the infinitely more friendly internet. The good old days are always just the old days.

Not everybody realizes that the Clash's "The Magnificent Seven," playing on both R&B and rock radio, is a rap song and a disco song. And not everybody in New York likes rap—far from it. WBLS loves to play the Police's "Voices inside My Head," though. I sometimes think this is the purest crossover record of all time.

The Mastodon Sweatshirt (2016)

The line connecting the security guard in subsidized housing, the Lassens checkout worker, and the start-up founder? Mastodon.

By wearing a Mastodon sweatshirt for eight years, I discover that Mastodon is America's band. I've never worn a piece of merch that prompts so many comments from such a diverse bunch of people.

Reading and Rapping (1983)

Mike Diamond is at St. Ann's, a year ahead of me. We are casual friends, not that tight. We are close enough to argue about the first Bad Brains tape and plan a zine but not close enough that we hang out in The City. The appeal of Beastie Boys is that they are an honest-to-god band and that is all I want out of life. I cannot seem to make this happen. New York is oddly thin on high school bands. They are more common on Long Island, where the garages have room for them.

In 1983, Beastie Boys release "Cooky Puss," a single that is related to rap, though it can also be taken as a parody of rap, just as the band is perceived as a parody of hardcore, which seems unfair to me at the time. This distance eventually proves useful. They've added Adam Horovitz to the band now that John Berry is gone. Both Adams—Horovitz and Yauch—lurk around St. Ann's and show up at parties.

Mike asks me to lend him the twelve-inch of the Treacherous Three's "Feel The Heartbeat." I tell him that he can just buy Taana Gardner's easier-to-find "Heartbeat" twelve-inch, but he wants the Treacherous Three version. This seems dumb. The Treacherous Three instrumental is just the Gardner song replayed by the Enjoy! house band. He isn't asking for the Beasties, though. He wants to record a song with the Beat Brothers: Tom Cushman, Tom Beller, and Mike. This is the first I am hearing of this!

The song they record, "Reading Rap," is straight outta PBS, musically rendered advice to read and stay in school. It is a cautionary tale, sort of like "White Lines" mixed with *Schoolhouse Rock!*, performed hesitantly over a drum machine and keyboard. The backing track sounds nothing like "Heartbeat" or "Heartbeat Rap," confirming my suspicion that Mike simply wanted that single and knew I would be naive enough to hand it over. (It has still not been returned.)

Reading and rapping, you'll be down, it's in the mix, hear it in the sound.

Hit the books, don't hit the street, and avoid the end that you might meet.

Cushman's two most famous appearances in public are being namechecked on *Paul's Boutique* in 1989 and being arrested for selling heroin to Philip Seymour Hoffman on the day of his death in 2014. The *New York Post* spells his name "Kushman" and he overdoses in 2019. He is the first of my St. Ann's friends to die.

A different but related moment is when Horovitz, excited, shows up at school with a test pressing of a record by T La Rock called *It's Yours*. It is the first record on Def Jam and distributed by Streetwise, a label I collect without exception. Adam is on the record, one of the party people chanting "Huh-o! Huh-o! Huh-o!" an early rap chant that might baffle people now. A person on a rap record—how the hell can you meet one of them? And then there one is.

What's exciting about this record is not that it is Rick Rubin's first rap production, or that Def Jam itself is starting, but that T-La Rock is the brother of LA Sunshine, one of the three members of the Treacherous Three, my favorite rappers. The most treacherous one, Kool Moe Dee, actually makes it out of the early, band-format days of rap and secures a spot in history by beefing with LL Cool J. This seems to matter when it happens.

New York college and commercial radio play what matters during my high school years. I assume payola and evil is running like a fever through these places, but they're spinning the records people actually love and it's a short hop when records move from the small stream to the bigger. WNYU has a hardcore hour called *Noise, the Show*, hosted by Tim Sommer, later of Hugo Largo, the man who signs Hootie & the Blowfish. The songs are generally shorter than a minute so I have to write out the J-card with a Rapidograph to fit in all the song titles. Rap radio starts on a station in Newark called WHBI, first with Mr. Magic, who moves to WBLS, where he hosts the first commercial rap show on New York radio, Thursday and Friday nights—the *Rap Attack*. Mr. Magic's slot on WHBI is filled by Afrika Islam and his *Zulu Beats* show, a looser and more historically informed affair. Islam's broadcast is fetishized by the English (who have always been good at isolating bits of American culture and expanding them into entire genres—e.g., "electro," which was just ten New York records, in New York).

There is breakdancing in the streets (a thing I am only OK at) and graffiti (a thing I can execute passably in small spaces). There are the clubs, most importantly. This change in NYC life can't be stressed enough. On a weekend, as kids, we go to Danceteria or Madam Rosa, later, simply to dance and hang out. The records I buy and play at home—like *The Dominatrix Sleeps Tonight* and the S.O.S. Band's *Just Be Good to Me*—are played at Danceteria in all their glorious sonic heft and at considerable volume. All of this is changed by the incursions of drugs into the clubs, the neutron bomb of AIDS, and the advent of Giuliani's fist politics and the cabaret laws. Economics shuts down enormous clubs like Danceteria and the World, home to Frankie Knuckles and New York's take on Chicago house music.

We lose the consensus that dancing is a default social activity and the idea that hip-hop is primarily dance music. All dance music ends up battling the abstractions of electronica, experienced at home or on headphones.

It isn't until 1986, my first summer living in New York, with a girlfriend, rather than at home, that the atomic bomb of hip-hop hits larger America. I return to school in the fall of that year as a junior at Brown. Over the summer, Tom has given me an advance cassette of Beastie Boys' *Licensed to Ill*. The J-card is printed red on white. The album is filled with breakbeats lifted from Islam's *Zulu Beats* show, old funk records that few outside New York would know (I think). What everyone knows is the opening beat for "Rhymin & Stealin," lifted from Led Zeppelin's "When the Levee Breaks."

The whole thing delights me. How did Led Zeppelin agree to something like this? What is anybody going to make of all these weird records and inside jokes? And why are Mike and Adam rapping about fucking someone with a whiffle ball bat? My assumption, for months, is that nobody outside the NYC club community will come close to getting it, and *Licensed to Ill* will be their third underground parody in a row.

When I come back from the summer, I live off-campus with Carla and Jen Fleming on Hope Street. It is one whole floor in a big, drafty wood home. Being out of the system, nominally, thrills me. Our house is on the north side of the campus. The walk from the Amtrak station takes me through most of the Brown campus, at the end of which lays a fraternity quadrangle. As I walk through the quad, I hear something familiar. At first, I assume my Walkman is still playing. Nope—*Licensed to Ill* is blasting from not one, not two, but three different windows. I stop and have something of an aphasic moment, a whiteout. It has not occurred to me—not even once—that "normal" people will like a rap album or any album by three weirdos from New York. I was planning to buy up *Licensed to Ill* as a cut-out, ten sealed copies at a pop. It turns out that I was not feeling the pulse of the nation.

That fall and winter, the four albums my heterodox household agrees on are *Licensed to Ill*, Bad Brains' *I*

Against I, Run-DMC's *Raising Hell*, and Scratch Acid's *Berserker*. We host a dance party and at the end of one, Tod Ashley from Dig Dat Hole is in the record room, playing "Perfection" over and over. I am not going to argue with Tod but I don't want to hear "Perfection" that many times.

I start another band. On my third try, I seem to get it right. I drop out of school.

Thievery (1983)

Trundling through a department store is my antsy mission, a minor terror. Later, during the nameless infirmity of teenage life, clerks mock and dismiss me and then, as if dragging anvils across their balls, point to records they know I can't afford. I don't see these as interactions but rocks that I climb to reach objects that might not betray me. I have a reoccurring query: What group are these clerks part of? If not mine, whose? There begins to be evidence that if I stick around, I can make one of these records and find the cohort that understands me. I will have to wait. These are mostly dance records with no images to match the sounds. I am wishing on dust.

At stores, rituals vary. In dance-music stores, the routine is to lift a vinyl single out of a basket on the wall. Then, you bring it to the DJ, who works at the front of the store, or in the back if the appropriate ceremony is to make the priest hard to find. A green adept-in-waiting, I am treated better by dance DJs than the guys who work at rock stores like Bleecker Bob's and Sounds. Do not underestimate this effect.

This all makes no commercial sense, as dance DJs have to play the records, a time-soak. If I end up buying anything, it is just a bag of twelve-inch dance singles retailing for $3.99 a pop. I rarely buy more than five. At rock-oriented stores, even if I buy used LPs and the tally is higher, I barely establish eye contact with a salesman who could have made me a member of whatever community I thought I was joining. Until college, outside New York, I can't remember one interaction in these stores, except for the time I am accused of stealing at J&R Music World.

I'm peeling a price sticker off a shrink-wrapped album, so that I can put it in the center of the corner, a relative idea. I hate mess and disorder and am worried it is going to fall off. Before I can finish my righting of the world, a lanky man with long hair who has seen me in the store about seven hundred times walks over and gargles, "You know, that's thievery." I haven't moved the record out of the bin or even noticed what record I am fussing with, so I just hear the word "thievery." This suggests that a grown man is spoiling for a fight with a teenager. I decide I should stick with Bondy's down the street and for a few weeks, I do. If he wants to shame me, he fails. I like being tidy. "Thievery"? Come on.

How Do You Feel About People (1996)

"Do you want kids? Well, you have people, you don't have kids. Same thing with revenue. A city doesn't generate revenue; it chooses investors. And when the highest bidder gets a seat, the highest bidder wins. And that is who owns New York now."

The Store Opens (1992)

On Grove Street, we live near a corner storefront on Bedford and Morton. I can't tell what it is. It's open, sometimes, but mostly not. Sometimes the hurricane gate goes up halfway and I can see that there's a restaurant in there, though it's more like a library and a restaurant combined. One day, the gate is more or less up. I poke my head in. There are people eating! It's less than half full at 2:00 p.m. Late for lunch, but fuck it, let's go. I've been shopping for music at Kim's on Bleecker Street, the one down the back of the video store. Jeff Gibson has probably put me on to a Hanatarash CD or something.

I venture past the doorway and one of the waitresses ushers me in. There are two of them, both cute as hell with short hair. I am seated in a booth and given a menu. There are hundreds of dishes, all listed in weak LaserJet-color ink. I get a chicken-salad sandwich with coleslaw on the side. It is all fresh and hot and cold and watery and perfect. Someone walks in and Kenny comes out from the back. He has curly grey hair and a big gut. His hair is kept back with a sweatband and he wears a black Shopsin's T-shirt.

"Get the fuck out!" he says to the new man. Goodbye, new man.

A decade later, the store moves to the corner of Bedford and Carmine, where it occupies a big space. Lots of windows! Candy bucket on the way out! No phones! No groups of more than four! Also, you can still get kicked out! Seems odd for it to be less protected, less socked away. Then it moves to a stall in Essex Market and Kenny dies.

The Rug + The Paper + The Ninas (1978)

Lying on the rug with the Sunday paper spread out, playing an album of Moog covers or a Beatles record or one of my ten forty-fives, looking for all the Ninas in the Hirschfeld drawings and reading every baseball stat. Manny Sanguillén!

Timing (1997)

When my father dies, my mother gives me his Honda Civic, a 1992 model. I have not been driving long. I don't get my license until 1995. Deborah's oldest friend, Matthew, teaches me how to drive. I take my first test in the Bronx and I fail because I apparently do not yield to pedestrians. I do not find this ruling fair or logical. The pedestrians in question were teens who surrounded my car as I crept along the streets of the Bronx. In what New York universe do you stop when surrounded by teens? Not the Bronx I tell you and not any other actual place. Matthew tells me to take the test in White Plains and I do and I pass.

The Honda is blue and thin, a rattling box. I love it. It has a stereo in it, for tapes only. I finally experience, at the age of twenty-eight, the thrill of listening to music in a car. This becomes a true gift in the rest of the decade, as we head into a high point for commercial hip-hop, each summer dominated by a new Jay-Z track. My children are raised going to Camp Mahackeno and listening to Foxy Brown and Tha Alkaholiks and Memphis Bleek. Sam, early on, takes a liking to Blur's "Song 2," which he calls "Hoo hoo."

But in June of 1997, when Deborah is nine months pregnant, we decide to flee New York for her parent's house in Weston, Connecticut. This becomes Deborah's house, more or less, after the divorce. For now, it is a house we are going to start using more, a house we are going to build an extension on to. We don't know when the baby is coming, but we are freaked out by caring for an infant in chaotic Lower Manhattan. The irony is that New York is one of the best places in the world to raise a small child. There are no drunk drivers, lots of friends and relatives to help, and everything is nearby.

We load up the Honda on a Friday night to drive. We have Deborah's parents' dog, Gable, and his son, Deacon, ours. Along with the dogs, there is all of my recording equipment, as well as my guitars and keyboards. The car sags with gear. We toodle up the Merritt Parkway as the gloaming hits. It's a nice drive.

We bank into a curve and something goes POPBBANG like metal hitting metal. The car becomes quiet and I notice the gas pedal no longer does anything. Ah, neat. Nothing is making the car move forward other than the momentum and our inertia. I instinctively drive onto the wide grassy embankment, not hitting the brake pedal, a gift I will never understand. We roll safely onto the grass and I turn the car off. Cars whip past but we are not in the line of traffic anymore. We both burst into tears.

A big supersized tow truck comes to get us and loads our car onto a flatbed. The timing belt broke, is what happened, and the repairs are much more expensive than I expect them to be. All of a sudden, late in the game, I am an American.

Trust (1980)

My mom gets me a ticket to see Elvis Costello and the Attractions on my thirteenth birthday. They are touring on *Trust* and I am sitting in the last row. It is a phenomenal show. Squeeze is the opening band. Words are cheerleading the instruments, forcing information to the center. The lyrics are leading to the riff that leads to the next part. It is two hours of pure force and connection, bit to bit, hook to hook, idea to idea. This is rock as paste, something so rich you could put it in water and make five other bands from it.

Food Restaurant (1988)

I am in an enfeebled version of my college band, Dolores, and working behind the counter of a restaurant called Food, a roomy spot on the corner of Prince and Wooster. I spend my spare money on records and live with one of my bandmates in Brooklyn, above a store on Flatbush called Royal Video.

Years later, I find out that Gordon Matta-Clark started Food, but all anybody knows at the time is that "a famous artist" invented the restaurant. The telephone game of history has turned the founder into Willem de Kooning.

The waiters are constantly pocketing the entire bill. Someone who works there shows me how to do it. I often take home an entire container of chicken salad after we close. If a homeless guy is outside when I leave, I give it to him. If he's not right there by the door, I get to keep it. This is one of a dozen superstitious games I play.

The Luthier (1999)

We play a show in Turin with the Sea and Cake, the first date of a short European tour. I forget to loosen the strings when loading my SG into checked baggage. This hold is not heated, so the strings contract and the notoriously weak SG neck splinters at the headstock. Sam Prekop lends me a black-and-white Jerry Jones Danelectro guitar for the show. The next day, we load up the van and drive to a luthier in central Turin. He glues and clamps my guitar, and hands it back to me like it is a bag of urine. His shop is filled with violins and cellos.

Blast First (1988)

At Food, I work with a tall, elegant woman with dyed-blond curls and ballet turnout—Joan. She is calm and hot and funny, and when it becomes clear that the restaurant is going to disintegrate, she does me a solid and puts in a word with her friends at the Blast First label on Mott Street. The only two employees are an English woman named Pat Naylor and Anne Lehman, an American. I am not paid but they give me free vinyl. They also give an advance cassette of *Daydream Nation*, red-and-white J-card. (It is manufactured by Enigma, because the two labels have teamed up for American distribution of Blast First, briefly.) It is the single best promo item I have ever received. Nothing else seems as much like a ticket to the magical ball. The album is, to my ear, about walking around New York in a daze, and I keep it in my Walkman, walking around New York in a daze, held in the golden orange center of time itself.

I am terrible at this job. They have an espresso machine, which is uncommon at that point. I do not yet drink coffee (I am twenty-one) and have never had cappuccino. I cannot master the foaming of milk or the making of black slurries. Other than that, I clip press articles and file them in folders. The artists don't tour much so there is not a great deal to do other than keep tabs on stock and look at the graveyard across the street. I'm pretty sure we are in the building on Mott that eventually became the Beasties' rehearsal-studio spot (down in the basement).

At some point, Anne and Pat want to make bookshelves, so I give them Craig Lively's number. Craig is the genius from Brown, leader of Clint Eastwood and United States of America. I pinch-hit in the former band and become a member of the latter, which lasts maybe three months. He is still the most talented person I've ever met and the handsomest. Trust me—there is still time for Craig Lively to become your hero. He looks like Harry Belafonte crossed with Lenny Kravitz, but bigger and prettier.

Craig works as a carpenter with his dad, so I know he can make the shelves. He does a stunning, detailed job and at least two people fall in love with him. The only bands that come in are Big Stick—super sweet and friendly—and Sonic Youth. I am so nervous about meeting Sonic Youth that I sit next to the window and pretend not to notice them when they come in. Very plausible. Lee comes over to say hello and is the sweetheart he always is. I do not speak to anyone else, out of pure terror. I do not embarrass myself because I do not do anything at all. You cannot knock this process sometimes.

September 11 (2001)

9/11

Trinidad (2015)

The man I work for talks about himself no matter what the topic. Basketball is Trinidad. Recycling is Trinidad.

Ride-sharing apps are Trinidad. He is constantly nervously reading aloud, grandstanding, threatening, bluffing, claiming he's "almost hired" everyone on both coasts, not knowing how to cut and paste, meaning that his assistant's big blocks of text stand out two points bigger than his own in the memos he "writes." He is always talking about a piece he wrote back home in Trinidad when he was nineteen, far before and beyond the reach of the internet, hell, maybe the piece was twenty thousand words long, maybe it was.

Robotron + LIC (1980)

I like video games when they are not anthropomorphic. I want to see spots and blocks and vectors. The swarming figures in *Robotron* make me anxious. I play to clean them up. I also love *Tempest*, all those angry vectors and sour-lemon lines.

Lamb with Mint Sauce (1980)

When I am thirteen, old enough to have some kind of consciousness, we go to see my grandparents in Kent. I also get to buy records in London, which seems a reason to travel. We are served lamb with mint sauce by their still-existing servant, who is called only "Nanny." Even though they apparently can't afford her, there she is. There is an entire set of my great-grandfather's books, all of them lightly moldy. Some are signed inside the front jacket "Yours, Edgar Wallace," which makes me wonder whom these books were originally given to. There are sheep outside. The collection I want most to bring home is my grandfather's Simenon collection, all of them original. They, too, are moldy. I don't like taking baths but I do it, as there are no showers. One bathroom is papered entirely with covers of an English gardening magazine. It's a good idea. The pull chain for the wooden toilet is an actual chain. It feels like the chain goes all the way to a point in an earlier century. Both my grandparents have completely white hair, and they are more funny than I expect.

Soundproofing (1983)

I come home at dawn, chest wide, clothes stuck to me after dancing out all the cheap speed and pot and beer. I slide into tight-cornered sheets, lying next to a wall covered with cardboard packaging that serves as an acoustic barrier between my room and my parents.

First Paycheck (1980)

I have my first paycheck from Eagle Printing in my pocket. I am on the corner of Dekalb and Washington Park. A man in camo pants and a white tank top appears out of nowhere and grabs me around the waist. He is up against me so close that I can't look up at him. It is a sunny day. He is holding a hunting knife to my stomach. I give him my check, which is all I have. *He's not named Alexander Jones! How will this work?* I go into Perry's, the deli on the corner of Dekalb and Carlton, and tell Perry. He comes out from behind the counter with an enormous kitchen knife. He walks up and down Dekalb for a while and then gives up.

Burn the Bun (1980)

My dad "almost dies" when I am thirteen. I am not mocking this moment, but asking you to understand that this event goes way into the red on the "What actually happened?" spectrum.

He appears at the top of the stairs one morning, leaning over the railing in his nightshirt and dramatically intoning, "I am bleeding internally." He goes to the hospital and we don't see him for a week. My mother comes into my room and sits on the bed with me and my brother, to tell us he might die. This doesn't seem helpful and I am never told exactly what is wrong.

He does not die, it seems, at all. He comes back and now knows he is diabetic. He quits drinking and smoking without any apparent difficulty. He is more cheerful and doesn't need to take insulin—he simply adjusts his diet. Any time I go to England for any reason, he asks me to get him diabetic chocolates at Boots. There are no obsessions in my dad's life except for this: diabetic sweets. Anything he can eat that doesn't have sugar is an instant hit. He eats lots of tuna fish and asks the waiter to "burn the bun, really black, like a mistake" when we get hamburgers anywhere.

London, Ontario (1999)

I am trying to get paid in London, Ontario. It is negative ten outside and my bandmates are no help. Actually, that isn't accurate. I've agreed to do this part of the job. They do a lot of lifting and driving. The division of labor is fair. The club owner doesn't want to pay us our guarantee because only nine people have paid to see Ui play. This, however, is exactly why bands have guarantees, so that it becomes worth it to leave home and travel all over the place doing shows for nine people. He pays me. My job, then, is simply to wait without flinching.

The Reading (1983)

When I win the Young Playwrights Festival, I am not necessarily a winner winner. I am a finalist. Three of us get full productions at the Public Theater, and the rest of us, about ten, get staged readings. That doesn't turn out to be the payoff—the preliminary reading is the best thing to happen. The cast? A guy who absolutely loved the play whose name I need to find, Željko Ivanek, and John Pankow. I am sixteen years old and these guys are reading my play. They're fantastic. I get a buzz stronger and more lasting than any I've gotten yet from doing some sort of art. When I wonder back to why I thought I was going into theater, I remember this. I made sense. The guy whose name I have forgotten, who plays the disabled criminal named Hampson, likes the play so much they do a second reading. This is heavenly shit and I hope, to this day, that I thanked everybody enough. I really hope I did.

The official staged reading is a huge letdown after this. Hampson is played by someone who overplays it and keeps buckling over like he needs to pee.

Kebab in Nottingham (1999)

After a gig in Amsterdam, we take a ferry to London and then drive up to Nottingham. We are all sick for most of the day, hungover and wrung out. Once in Nottingham, we have to hump our gear up a fire escape to get it into the church, where we will be playing on a tiny stage. We don't fit but we play with intensity and bond with the local opening band. We all get kebabs after the show and I complete the band hat trick by throwing up afterward. Touring still feels worth it.

Secure the Bag (1984)

Any time somebody in a movie leaves their bag somewhere, or drops it, I think predominantly about that bag for the rest of the scene. Still true.

A Writer (1979)

My father tells me I am a writer, in a way that he wishes he was. He is paid to be a copywriter for ad agencies. I am twelve.

Withdrawal (2015)

I approach my withdrawal from this drug like a mental phenomenon, mostly because I assume my brain will be sensing my brain, but the process is more like a physical restoration. When the meniscus in my right knee was torn, and was then repaired by a surgeon, a doctor told me that it would take about six months to heal. The healing took closer to eighteen months. With this kind of recovery, there are not many benchmarks. Day to day, it feels like nothing is happening, leading to panic. Then time passes. When I finally felt like a person without a knee problem, enough time had passed that I had given up feeling like I would not be a damaged person. But knee recovery is not the inverse of anything. Not taking a drug is the inverse of taking a drug. So it surprises me that anyone ever stops taking a drug. The drug works in seconds. Sobriety kicks in long after you become sober.

The Kiosk (2014)

After the festival, a few hung-over booking agents and music writers start back to New York. Our flight from Krakow to Warsaw takes off on time, which we do not expect. I don't think about the money I am carrying. Once we arrive in the Warsaw airport, an hour after leaving Krakow, I find an exchange kiosk staffed by two employees. It is bright inside like an operating theater. Its roof is pointed and striped with blue and red. Maybe they sell snow cones during lulls. A clerk looks at me through the

Plexiglas. I realize I am exchanging only five or ten zlotys for American currency. Does this amount to anything? Nope. Performing a familiar deed in an unfamiliar language, I ask for a dollar. The clerk announces, "Dollar! Dollar!" alerting me to the fact that I am a beggar. His pale-green shirt crimps and he turns to laugh at his coworker. I want to give him back the dollar but I need it.

We Three Kings (1983)

I'm not good at talking. People ask me what my play is about. I want to say, "I'm sixteen. I don't know." I write *We Three Kings* in a dopey rush, on a manual typewriter handed over by my father. (I bug him about it, as with every typewriter he has, until he gets a new one, always a castoff from whichever ad agency he is working for.) "It's about three criminals living in a basement," is what I say. "It's violent and depressing." It takes me decades to realize I am processing the murder of my friend's mother.

I read Pinter, Albee, and Mamet, in a chronological, encyclopedic churn that I still lapse into when excited. My play owes them all eighty cents on the dollar. Their work is keyed to rhythms of talking, the pauses and fragments you can't avoid without a speechwriter. My teenaged concept is that no play is more realistic than any other but whatever you write should be pulled from a verifiably human source. Pinter makes bricks out of the vernacular and Mamet makes sharp edges sharper. Albee sounds to me like what you would say normally, followed by everything you're thinking but not saying. I'm attracted to the unpleasant aspects of all this language, as well as plays by Ionesco and Jarry. Anyone who confuses me enough to convince me they know something I don't appeals to me.

Shakespeare's plays have no relationship to verisimilitude, so there is no reason to worry about how his characters speak. When I am in *Romeo and Juliet*, I just memorize the words and wait for the patterns to kick in. Playwrights like Eugene O'Neill confuse me. His work from the recent twentieth century has no relationship to my reality. The lines sound like they've been lifted from assembly at some morbid high school: everything orated, nothing spoken.

The Blue Feather (2008)

I am dating an aerialist named Garbanza. Her apartment is one and a half times taller than a normal apartment so she can climb up chains and practice every morning. She comes to my house and brings her cat, Motherwell, named after Robert. I leave the window open and Motherwell jumps out, on the twenty-third floor, and clambers up. The doorman calls me to say that a woman is running around on the roof with a blue feather. The people across the street think she's a jumper. It is Garbanza, looking for her cat. Afterward, we have an almost verbatim *Sex and the City* conversation on the train.

"I know it seems now like I'm one of those women!"

We never see each other or speak again.

Crying Semiprivate (2013)

I don't know how loud my crying is until the anniversary of my father's death. I say goodbye to Sam, close the door, and see the calendar. I don't notice that I have started crying again. After months of doing it in public, crying indoors feels as if it is silent. Five minutes after Sam leaves, he returns, crying, because he heard me from the street. In another situation, I would be embarrassed or think of being embarrassed. We stand in my living room and hold each other, almost the same height.

Haus of Ouch (1993)

For a couple of years, Ui rehearses in David Linton's loft on Baxter Street, in Chinatown. It's two blocks from our loft on Broadway and Walker. The loft is at the top of a building mostly taken up with Chinese commerce. It's a great space—lots of rickety, splintering wood and big windows looking out on to Canal Street. We eat lots of phở from around the corner. Dave Reid's band, Wider, rehearses here, as do Envelope and Blonde Redhead. Linton starts putting on a Haus of Ouch night, where bands play and I spin records in between sets. This is the first time I use the name Calvinist, which I still use. It's all very informal and fun, no downsides. When I hear some of the older musicians there being bitter about Sonic Youth's success, I vow never to become like that. There will obviously be no money, so why would I choose to play music and land on some ghost resentment and grouch out?

The illbient scene is heaving into view, and some of their shows happen at Linton's space. I don't tend to DJ on the nights when the performers are also DJs, though nothing is particularly set. On one night, a famous actor and saxophonist shows up, which is exciting. He comes with two women and complains about the five-dollar entry fee. Once inside, he unscrews two of the red bulbs we've put in and leaves almost immediately.

"Heroes" (2017)

Deborah and Van go on a romantic trip to Poland during her sophomore year and part to the strains of "Heroes." It is a story that, by osmosis, becomes my memory. Very little makes Deborah cry, but "Heroes" does. We always have to turn it off when it comes on. Eventually, I cry when I hear the song in public.

Our marriage ends and the college boyfriend returns, eventually marrying Deborah. Because Deborah's memory had overwritten my own—had become mine—I realize that there could be no accurate version of remembering. There is no such thing. And after a few weeks of thinking I had never seen Bowie, I remember that we did, at Jones Beach, exactly three weeks before he suffered a heart attack on stage and stopped playing live.

Wisdom Teeth (1997)

It's a Friday and I am on the way to get a molar yanked. I've delayed the procedure for over a year because: teeth, pulling, fuck that. It is a Friday morning, close to noon. The phone rings. Deborah answers and hands me the receiver. It is my mother. My father has been readmitted to a hospital in Gloucester. On Wednesday, he is sent home after a back operation but faints, and is brought back in. He and I speak several times before that Friday. I haven't thought much about why he'd faint after being released from a hospital. There has been mention of a "blood clot," which sounds benign, a thing you can pull apart with your hands. He sounds like himself over the phone, cheerful. It never crosses my mind to wonder what can happen if a clot enters the heart.

I take the receiver from my wife. My mother explains that my father has experienced a heart attack an hour earlier. While she is telling me this, he has another. There is a brief pause and I hear the cloaked sound of someone talking over a weak network in the middle of ambient noise. It sounds a bit like wind knocking over a bunch of leaves. My mom gets back on the phone and tells me that he is gone. My father is dead. I cancel my tooth extraction and get on a plane to Boston.

Two days later, I deliver a eulogy after several people in my family tell me they can't. The day before the service, my godfather, Uncle John, tells me over a phone that he can't make it to the service. My feet go cold in my black leather dress shoes. I look at the vaguely Turkish, ugly carpet underneath the table, holding the phone as he pauses and pauses and then says the wrong thing. I think of that moment every time someone tells me they can't do something.

When I speak at the service, it is the first time I've said anything about my father since his death. I am standing in front of people and this is not the best place to recall his words and ways. I start to cry, but an internal lock cinches, fixing my muscles so that I can say words as I think of them. I remember none of what I say, just that when I am done, I sit seen and unseen.

Albert (1983)

I don't know why Albert spends time with me. He never hits on me or makes money by talking to me. Is he kind? Bored? Does he like the idea of me replicating his taste? Years later, when he disappears, and other people at the store look at me as if I am stranded, I know I've lost a connection to a culture. I don't know if it is the culture that births hip-hop. I know it is a culture. At the time, it is just Albert's.

Hip-hop is called "rap" and is represented by records in the back of the store that only a few people want to hear. Nobody is banging on about culture and realness or anything abstract. I stumble onto one guy—the only one I claim—who is part of something nameless but developing. Without meaning to perform an historical immersion, he takes me through the records that become the alphabet of hip-hop. Neither of us know this is going on.

The first time I go to Downtown Records, it is still located on Sixth Avenue, right above Twenty-Third Street. The store, confusingly, is not downtown, mirroring another rap mecca, Downstairs Records, which is upstairs.

My friend Tom tells me this is the spot. I'm looking for a twelve-inch of Nona Hendryx's "Transformation." Before finding the Nona record, I am distracted by a series of multicolored records, all with the same illustration on the label: an octopus, smiling and playing seven turntables at once. I assume it is worth buying a bootleg record promoted by an octopus.

This series is standardized and expanded into the *Ultimate Breaks & Beats* series, an unofficial Bible of hip-hop samples that maintains authority by getting there first. Whether or not these songs are included because they've been sampled or vice versa is never clear. In the later volumes, it seems most likely that label owner, Lenny Roberts, has introduced a song into the series because it is being widely sampled. When the series begins, sampling isn't technically possible (that's more like 1986) but the series is defining a canon: "Apache," "Handclapping Song," "Nautilus," and so on. By the time the series reaches a twenty-fifth volume, samples are the core of hip-hop. Soon enough, sampling is an ancient tradition with little place in new rap records.

As I sort through the octopus records and consider how to spend my twenty dollars, Albert yells at me from the DJ platform, which is a small white wooden riser in the back of the store. He yells, "Over there!" and points to a vertical wire rack that holds twenty LPs in baskets, five to a side. The rack is filled with sealed copies of the first RCA Jimmy Castor Bunch album, *It's Just Begun*, released in 1972. The corner of each LP jacket is snipped off. "Buy two," he says. They are $3.99 each. I say, "OK," because I am fairly sure that "It's Just Begun" is this breakneck song that I'd heard on WHBI, the one with the hyperactive bassline and screaming and a cowbell pattern that sounds like Morse code. Yes, that is the song, yes yes yes yes.

Albert is not warm or avuncular. He could be taking pity on me, though that idea doesn't hold much water. He is irritable, maybe because of coke, a drug I know nothing about except that Tony Montana has a pile of it on his table. Tony Montana is very irritable. Unless he's busy, Albert plays me records. When I can't get his attention, our flimsy bond is not even a memory.

Whether or not he is recommending an album is not always clear. He crouches down, pulls a piece of vinyl from a crate, and plays it while cueing something else up. There is no eye contact between us, so what he is doing is always possibly something he is doing for himself. I can only sense the intention when he looks at me, after minutes of playing a song, and says, "That's the shit."

Albert is not like other record clerks. With few exceptions, the record store people I deal with are surly mushrooms with no interest in helping people. Are they misanthropes? Do they mimic misanthropes? Something about the arrangement has killed their empathy so that they see customers as stupider and more corrupt than the people I have to serve when I work as a sandwich maker or waiter. This makes no sense, as service jobs seem to offer equal opportunities to be humiliated.

But it is different to record store clerks; they go to work in record stores because they care about music and need money. Encountering people who don't care about music in the same way, or the right way, seems disappointing to them in a way that goes way past botheration. Clerks are one of the first cohorts I see forming around musical taste, and yet they end up choosing the sting of resentment rather than the glue of love. They don't stick with each other or us! They also don't necessarily know what their taste is or even what cohort they are a part of, only that the people who come into their stores and ask for top ten records are somehow betraying The Cause and making them Work rather than be Spirit Guides, a job they resent despite never trying to do it. Weak idealists make strong cynics.

You're selling widgets when you sell records, but that doesn't mean records don't matter at a spiritual level. You could keep a friend afloat by selling his record, or change a stranger's life by introducing them to Can. Indifference to these agendas is what makes the job suck. With pay so low, the gig can become a dystopia where nobody is being converted to any cause and nobody is paying the rent. The clerks then feel like postal workers on the smallest block in town, where everybody knows what packages they're getting already. The clerk becomes a carrier pigeon, a hinged panel in an inefficient conveyor belt.

That doesn't make me sympathetic to their shrugging. I am not impolite to people asking for sandwiches or to the suited jagoffs who want their packages to move more quickly between Long Island City and Manhattan when I'm working as a messenger. Because I sense that clerks have turned their surliness (born from hurt) into a badge of honor, I dread every trip I make to record stores. As I go to record stores almost daily between the ages of ten and forty, I live through a lot of weak dread.

Downtown Records is caught in the gap between a fading dance community, largely gay, and the rap community, straight and younger, but not yet convinced that they are a community. We buy records from any camp. It is not clear which songs belong to which camp or what any of us is signing up for.

At stores like Downtown, you gather records and hand them to a person who can play them for you. At stores like Vinylmania, on Carmine Street, this person is likely a DJ first and a salesman second. In Times Square, on Sixth Avenue, and in Midtown, whoever is working plays the records. This job is just work, not a chance to demonstrate skills. The process can take half an hour. When it's all done, the employee rarely says anything.

On one slow high school afternoon, I ride my bike from Brooklyn into Manhattan, all the way to the store. Albert brings me behind the decks and starts playing records. There are a few customers around, socializing and buying things. These people could be part of my cohort if Albert failed me.

Albert plays Mandrill's "Mango Meat," bungee-cord guitars and tide-pool horns over subcutaneous bumps. It's familiar and unknown. It is slow in a way that I like, because it's easier to dance double time over slower beats, at least for me. When he plays me a single from

Samba Soul made in 1977, a disco cover of "Mambo No. 5," I'm challenged. To me, someone ignorant of Afro-Cuban music, the record seems old. Someone has turned an old-people tune into a disco song, which is already an old genre in the eighties. Disco is too fast. But this is different—I hear live drums and congas and a bass guitar. When the song switches between the horns and the rhythm section, it sounds like teens are playing along with their parents. Whoever made this song can feel what is coming, a kinetic beast that will start at disco and go beyond it.

The Radio (1983)

The radio matters more than any other tool for discovering music. By 1990, I've stopped listening to the radio entirely.

Price Points (2017)

Who the fuck knows what steak costs. The price point is some bullshit.

Buying Singles at A+S (1976)

There are glories in our age and the barriers are taller than the glories. If you love music, you have to fight for it. This conflict can be romanticized as a value exchange, as if inaccessibility always indicates the presence of precious qualities. It doesn't. Struggling to find records didn't make them better. The value of effort changes when it comes to making records, though, and that's another story.

For a kid in the seventies, records didn't have names. Listeners were at the mercy of radio DJs. They might say the names of the records they played, once, before or after you'd tuned in. There was no choice but to get lucky. Music leaked through cracks and left us to find it. Maybe that "Dance, Dance, Dance" song from a roller disco came from the place where a man played the organ and welcomed us back, his friends, to a show that never ends.

When I learned names, it was hard to find anyone who wanted to sell me records attached to those names. How much could a kid buy? Without a bankrolling parent, kids were just loiterers.

In seventh grade, my best friend John told me he had gangrene and a synthesizer. He had only one of these things. I didn't care that he lied about the gangrene because I lied about being a detective. I wanted a stereo like his, and permission to play records as loud as he could. His parents were actors. Did volume not bother actors? Were they deaf because of stage explosions? My parents were in a choir, so maybe that was relevant—choirs weren't nearly as loud as explosions. I had friends whose parents let them smoke pot at home, but that was a dead end. I liked being high only in places outside of daily life, beyond a schedule.

In the seventies, you could make a radio from parts not because you were a wizard but because it was cheaper and easier to make gear from Heathkit than to go to a chain store, and New York had few chain stores. Technology wasn't of note unless it could take you to the moon. Nobody was going to be impressed because you built a fucking radio.

If music was going to be ours, and not just atmospheric frustration, it had to heave up and claim coordinates like a star system. It had to become findable. We had our radios and turntables but we weren't going to wait indefinitely. Where did it all come from?

My green-and-white plastic phonograph opened outward, like a suitcase, and wasn't very good at being an appliance. It could pull in one radio station, WABC 770 AM.

Before I figured out that I could buy a copy of a song I liked, radio determined the music I heard. If music wasn't on the radio, it wasn't there. It didn't occur to me that I could go and get my own copies of these things. The albums that my parents lent me sat on the turntable like mushrooms on a plank. The measurements of my plastic stereo seemed off. The plastic tonearm was stranded on the edge of the vinyl, drifting toward a center. It all looked like a failed prototype for a can opener. I assumed the needle would skid, but the hairy spiral pulled out music, every time.

One day, I walked out onto our stoop on South Portland Avenue. I wanted to buy records. I asked my mother, "Why are the records in the back of a department store?"

I had to walk through the women's underwear department at A&S to buy a record. I was nine. Once I had established a path, the habit of visiting a person at the same time every day, there wasn't much to do but wait for my allowance to build up and then make the trip. Soon, I learned that going to live shows was easier. You'd get in or not. A bad show didn't shake my faith in anything beyond the band or the venue. Records, though, felt like a tangle I couldn't get out of. I felt, early on, like I was supposed to be in that tangle and live there until I got out with a haul.

Anything distant from me was *pop*. Something in the neighborhood was *punk*. Those are the terms of the eighties, though, and in retrospect it all feels like a struggle about access. If something had been easier to find than something else, I probably would have loved it. That was why I loved every song on the jukebox at Blimpie on Montague Street. Talk about clearly labeled.

Nice Jazz (1987)

John Corbett scores me a gig at WBRU, playing the jazz slot from midnight to 6:00 a.m. I live in Providence this summer, seeing my girlfriend Brenda, and drifting along thinking about the band and thinking about writing. I am technically not a student anymore. It is a summer that elapses almost entirely a foot or two above the earth. When I hear "chill out" and "man, just living life," I think that I have only done this once and it is this summer.

Even though I am twenty years old and indestructible, I cannot stay up all night very easily. This job does not pay so I do not construct my life around it. My strategy is to zoom around through bop and small bands and current stuff and then save my album-length tracks for the period after 3:00 a.m. My taste runs hard toward energetic, free players, so there are lots of Ayler and Cecil Taylor and Arista Freedom albums like Julius Hemphill's *Coon Bid'ness*, which I play almost every week. My lifesavers are the Art Ensemble of Chicago tracks that take up a whole side. We are a little bit before the CD era, so there are a few of them, but not many jazz titles. A twenty-minute side allows me to sort of catnap, a little. The machine downstairs has RC Cola. The rock side of the camp has a few weird new titles, like Swans and Camper Van Beethoven, which I tape in the funny smaller studios.

Almost every time I DJ, a man calls. After a quick reminder of his name, he says, slow and not that upset,

"Why don't you play some nice jazz?" I imagine that he has trouble changing the dial on his radio, and maybe has trouble sleeping. I feel for him—and though there is a lot of squeaking in my sets, there is plenty of Monk and Bird, too.

Bat Day (1980)

On June 23, my brother, my parents, and I return from Burger King Bat Day at Yankee Stadium. We have collected nine bats. Why is anyone allowed to leave a baseball stadium with nine bats? Tabloids won't shut up about how violent New York is, but here they are, nine baseball bats obtained without any qualification beyond thumbs. Looking at them stuffed into the umbrella stand like asparagus in a pencil cup, I imagine I'll have to distribute them along Carlton Avenue. No need. Someone breaks a pane in our front door and jacks all but two. The next day, I play with the kids on the block, all of them with new bats.

Who Speaks for You? (1989)

After an argument about a girlfriend and a mutual acknowledgement of my unsteady future, my father asks me, "Who speaks for you?"

I wish someone had taught me about savings and cooking. It is odd that nobody does, and then, after time, odder that I don't teach myself. In sobriety, I teach myself both of these things, slowly. Faith is not panicking, a friend of mine tells me.

Playing the Wall (1986)

The first free-jazz show I see is drummer Han Bennink and saxophonist Peter Brötzmann. They play a small recital hall on campus. The room seats about fifty or so and is lined with acoustic wood paneling, the good stuff classical people get, nonparallel surfaces to defeat those standing waves. I know nothing about free improvisation. Later, John and I go to other shows in Boston, like Ed Blackwell and Dewey Redman. (We also see the Jesus and Mary Chain play on a barge in Boston.) I've only seen a few traditional jazz concerts at this point and I don't know the differences between jazz and improv and free improv, or if there are any.

Brötzmann is a big, walrus person who tries to extrude his brains through his tenor saxophone. He blows with a digestive fury and a broken, crying tone, a bit like Albert Ayler playing tenor. Han Bennink plays his drum set with thin sticks and is very tall. Everything is life or death to Brötzmann and a mad joke to Bennink. Eventually, Bennink stops playing his drum kit and stands up. He walks around the hall, thrumming and paradiddling the wall, and then the fire extinguisher.

I can tell how seriously these people take their craft and how little they care for propriety. They play their asses off in every sense, and though their music is not the kind I want to play, I want to be connected to their sense of aliveness and attention with everything spun fresh in the moment.

Kids' Liberation Army (1977)

In 1977, I am brought to the principal's office for inciting violence. My friend Dave and I have been seeing TV reports about Patty Hearst and the Symbionese Liberation Army. It seems obvious that this is the way to go—determine your cause and rob a bank. Choose a cool name, wear a cool uniform. In the lower school library, where middle schoolers like us technically do not belong, Dave and I work on outfits for the Kids' Liberation Army. We aren't angry. We simply think the SLA people are cool and have cool uniforms, like baseball players or *Star Wars* characters.

I draw the yellow KLA outfits in a graph-paper notebook with felt-tip markers. Stanley Bosworth's wife, Annie, is the librarian in the main library, which is two stories tall and stationed on the fourth floor. I'm not sure who is in charge of the lower school library, a modest little cavern on the third floor. Someone rats us out and we have to go explain ourselves.

Pay to Cum (1980)

I hear a punk song on the radio. It is called "Pay to Cum," by a band called Bad Brains. I don't know how the day goes. I don't have a Walkman. They are expensive enough to be above the level of things my parents can buy. This means that, aside from music coming out of the television before I go to school and a tape playing in the high school smoking lounge, no music reaches me between 7:00 a.m. and my coming home at 4:30 p.m. When I get home, I tune into *The New Afternoon Show* on WNYU, a college station show I can pull in because we have moved from Fort Greene to the edge of Brooklyn Heights and aligned ourselves with a clear radio connection to Manhattan.

Imagine the day. You've gone about your teenaged business for nine hours without hearing any prerecorded audio. After a gap, you turn on a device that drives a signal into bad speakers. What you hear is like a water main bursting. Over the rush, a man recites the table of elements so quickly that it sounds like the tape is being advanced by hand. Water fills space. It is clear that this is music, a band playing instruments. You forget that your front door keys are still in your hand. You haven't thought to put a cassette in the recorder and press a button to record the moment so that it becomes yours, a thing to use. The song is over before you know what to feel. Nothing happens all day and then everything happens and it has no name.

Blimpie + Sledgehammers (1976)

The coolest place on Montague Street in 1976 is a Blimpie. Blimpie sandwiches were then, as they are now, made on ever-so-slightly-too-light hero bread with lots of oil and vinegar, shredded iceberg, thinly sliced meats, and so on. Roast beef is my religion for years.

The point of being at Blimpie is that the cool kids, the loafs in their army jackets, are also there. There is a jukebox in the back, near the bathroom. I don't remember who the cool kids are—probably Jeff Tischler and Genji Siraisi are there—but I remember playing Boston's "More Than a Feeling." Having the quarter to play it is only part of the triumph; I have managed to overcome my internal prohibition against passing by the Loafs Table and dropping the quarter in. The Loafs do not tease me or my friend, and it is worth mentioning that if there is teasing and bullying at St. Ann's, it is light. (In my experience.)

I am there for twelve years, and despite the school having turned into a platform for celebrity children romping through a multisite donor complex, the school absolutely cares for me and keeps me safe and warm and happy. Hundreds and hundreds of odd kids, only about half of them rich, are able to cultivate whatever makes them feel like people. The teachers I have are almost uniformly smart and attentive and caring and without pretense. We have a smoking lounge, for fuck's sake—obviously the administration cares about us.

We have a sandbox and a garden in the backyard at South Portland and life feels good, logical, boring. But we have tasks I never quite understand. We remodel the basement ourselves, which is great fun. We put on face masks and take sledgehammers to a wall, watching plaster and lathing pile up. We go on Saturday trips to Pintchik on Flatbush, picking up paint. The machine that shakes the paint is compelling. It also appears in *Saturday Night Live*. Would a leading character now work in a paint store?

Our attic is full of rubble. There are two entire rooms up there that go unused, which seems nuts in 2020. I am sure it was in 1975, too. My parents install a rope swing in the attic, which pulls out of the ceiling one day. My first thought isn't "Why did they let me do that!" but "We need to secure this with some kind of anchor."

I also play in a demobbed dumbwaiter shaft, which I childproof with cardboard. I get used to protecting myself. It is fun, and I am grateful that my parents let me do so many dumb, dumb things.

Hired (2004)

In 2003, Alex Ross alleges that Justin Timberlake might not own a pen, in the *New Yorker*. (Ross's column is not, in large, about Timberlake.) This is before Twitter, when people have to learn Movable Type and start a blog if they want to argue. I take issue with Ross's take in a column for *Slate*.

Alex doesn't send me a diatribe in response. His email is eloquent and friendly. He disagrees with a point I've made about Adorno but is gracious enough to admit that maybe he has underestimated Timberlake's skills as a songwriter. This exchange begins a friendship that is still vital to me.

In 2004, I get a call from David Remnick. He asks if I have time to come in and see him.

I show up in his office on my birthday, a Friday in January. I'm so nervous that I sit on a framed photo of Václav Havel (or someone who looks like Havel). I ask Remnick if I can take a picture of the old *New York Times* building, the top of which is visible from his office. As he often will, Remnick spreads his hands, as if to reassure a lost tourist that he has not, in fact, walked twenty blocks in the wrong direction. He says, "You'll be back. Don't worry."

My piece on Arthur Russell is the first column. I have weeks to write and revise it. All I do in those weeks is draft. Some of Russell's unreleased work is being put out by the

Audika label, so I have a chance to write about someone who is gone—Russell died of AIDS-related complications in 1992—but also central to my life. Remnick puts me in the hands of John Bennet, a Texan who becomes my horse whisperer. There are only a few editors on the planet as good as Bennet. His touch is so gentle and his advice so carefully considered that you rarely feel the scalpel. After working together for a year, Bennet says, "I always cut your first two paragraphs. They're just throat-clearing."

I email my piece to Bennet on a Friday, assuming that I will have to wait until Monday for an answer. Bennet emails me on Saturday morning to tell me that the piece is good enough to run. I have written three columns for the magazine when a journalist emails me a question to the effect of "What the hell are you doing at the *New Yorker*?" I email Remnick and ask him what I should say. He writes back, "We'd be delighted if you told them you're the pop critic." The audition is over.

I write back to the reporter, take the elevator downstairs and walk out onto Forty-Third Street. My father brought me up on collections of work written by *New Yorker* staffers: S. J. Perelman, Joseph Mitchell, A. J. Liebling, James Thurber. I look up and down the street, imagining what Perelman might say about the LED screens to my left or the Starbucks across from me. I realize, while standing on Forty-Third Street, that my father will never know about this job. At that point, I am not the writer he'd always hoped I would become. I am an office drone playing in an instrumental-rock band that my father tolerated, at best. I walk into Starbucks and try to buy a juice. I can't speak my order and step out of the line. A woman offers me a handkerchief. I thank her and go back upstairs. I email Bennet and ask him if the magazine would be OK with my going to England to write about a new singer who has one song out, a single called "Galang." He writes back, "OK."

I go to see M.I.A.'s first New York appearance in a Chelsea loft, a show sponsored by either a clothing company or a liquor company. M.I.A. and her dancer, Cherry, perform on the floor, with the crowd circling them. They play four or five songs—no more.

When I go to meet with Maya in London, we are both new to being professionals. Over the course of two days, we walk around and she tells me about her life in Sri Lanka and in London. She talks in the kind of detail that performers rarely risk now.

I see her again, in 2014, when we tape a video segment for the magazine's website. She hugs me and says, "God, it's been ten years." Then she says, "You were wrong, though. I never said I was sorry." She is referring to a blog post, from 2012, titled "M.I.A. Shouldn't Have Apologized." After she gave the middle finger at the Super Bowl, a piece quotes someone in her camp as saying that she regrets the gesture. I link to that piece. It seems like an appropriately M.I.A. moment to meet up and get fact-checked. She is right.

The Mariah Carey column also sticks out, for several reasons. The assignment comes about when Remnick stops me in the hall and says, "Why don't you write about that shrieking woman?" *The Emancipation of Mimi* has been out for almost a year, so there's lots of time to absorb the music and watch the album devour the charts. It is a real blessing to have a year's time to think before writing about an album, and the magazine affords that (though usually the idea is to strike when something is now). The column also typifies our largely peaceful editorial consensus, which is to vary what genres appear in the column. Pop stars and noise-makers are treated equally and I come as close to having no dog in the fight as is possible at Condé Nast (which is not that close). I get to see Mariah live, who is so comfortable performing in a nightgown that Madison Square Garden shrinks and becomes her living room.

When I interview Bill Withers for a column, he is at home, in Los Angeles. I love his first four albums as much as I love any recorded music. He is cordial for only three minutes. As soon as we start talking about the 1980s, when he signed with Sony, his mood dips. I ask something vague about "Just the Two of Us," a song he wrote with Grover Washington Jr., which was released in 1981, with Washington listed as the main artist. Withers doesn't like that topic, so I suggest that we talk about something else. Withers says, "This conversation sucks. I'm going to take a shower." It's a good line and I use it now.

The Tom Waits column is the beginning of the end. My recording options have failed so when Waits and I talk on the phone, I tell him I have to transcribe his words by hand. The fact-checkers will call to confirm that he said what we think he said. Four times, Waits asks, "How do I know you're getting this right?" I quit, in 2015, because I no longer know what "right" means in this context and I need to get sober before I simply fall over and die.

Knock on the Available Doors (1994)

Deborah loves Double XX Posse's "Not Gonna Be Able to Do It." This song is on one of the bootleg cassettes I buy on Seventh Avenue when we work in the same office. Someone grabs the commercial release and dupes up several hundred to sell the week of release. These cassettes cost four dollars, sometimes five. They sound OK and I make myself feel better by buying the corresponding CD when I have transgressed with a bootleg. Since those CDs are coming from press people selling their advances, I am not, in fact, helping the artist. Sorry, posse!

Deborah is convinced that the chorus of the song is "knock on the available doors," which is now what this song is to me. Sorry, posse!

Peel + Ui (1993)

John Peel plays the first Ui EP on his BBC radio show. Over the course of a month or two, he plays all seven songs on the EP. The record is released only in England, on vinyl, which turns out to be a suboptimal decision. Justine Wolfenden puts out the record on her label, Hemiola, after seeing us play at a club called Brownies at 169 Avenue A, right below Eleventh Street. This becomes a bar called Hi-Fi and then a club called Heaven Can Wait.

When Justine and I talk about the record, we informally refer to it as "The Disco Bag" twelve-inch, because we both love twelve-inch, forty-five-RPM singles, largely for reasons of audio fidelity. The recording, originally intended to yield maybe three songs, blooms into a three-day session that leaves us enough material for an album. We winnow that down to seven songs and stick with the vinyl-EP idea.

We discover in the fall of 1993 that publications do not like to review EPs. *Where is the album?* they ask. CDs are taking off and imports seem to be losing their cachet. We are two years away from releasing a full album, meaning we will be time-stamped for some as debuting in 1995, even though we start playing live shows in 1991. "Optics," they call these things.

We find out about Peel because Justine's boyfriend, Keith, tapes the Peel shows and kindly sends me cassettes from England. Peel's nod feels like the highest vindication, since he ignores plenty of bands and is never wrong. (My failure to love happy hardcore as much as Peel is just that—a failure that time will hopefully heal, as I learn to love this insanely fast and upbeat dance music.) The frustration that comes because nobody's heard of the band and the warmth that comes from Sir John's benediction suggests that I should not look for too much nor beg too many times. A band is a series of joyful and brief moments that may not support an entire life but cannot be underestimated. Musicians who are bitter seem to think they have been cheated out of something because some other person did not raise their music up higher. The pickling can be avoided by being glad when anybody at all likes your music. Also: keep your day job.

Shoplifting at Lamson's (1978)

In the summer of 1978, I am an eleven-year-old back at Packer Day Camp. My younger brother, Tobias, also attends. After a day's activities, usually floor hockey and loitering in the courtyard and eating peanut-butter-and-pickle sandwiches, I take Tobias home on the B38 bus. I love Packer Day Camp. I am thrilled nobody has sent me to some camp in the woods. I do not want to jump off a tire swing into a creek. There are no baseball cards in the woods.

On this day, I decide to take him down the block to the Lamson's on the corner of Court Street and Joralemon. It's a big sort of Kmart all-purpose shop, a chain store local to the Northeast. I've been going there in the afternoon to buy candy and boost three-packs of baseball cards. I wear a green baseball jacket, cinched at the wrists and waist with stretchy green fabric. My routine is to slide one of these thin-boy three-packs up my sleeve, and it's been working.

This day is different. While I'm trailing Tobias around, both of us with metal lunch boxes, I get a feeling. I steal one three-pack and then another. I feel warm and strange. The card racks near the cash register are mostly ignored. Up on the mezzanine are the cheap plastic toys and I rarely visit them because I don't have the money. Today, something is new and wrong and nagging me. I walk up the stairs, leaving Tobias on the lower floor, unattended. I've started fiending. It's my first run.

I tent my jacket over my arms while I slide toys into the space beneath. I grab toy pistols, soft-pink Spaldeens, green-plastic soldiers, enough loot that distinct corners appear through my jacket. I can feel people watching me and yet I do not stop. I am warm and red and yet I continue. I know.

I walk downstairs and find Tobias, who looks worried. We walk through the front door and not three feet onto the sidewalk, I feel a hard hand on my shoulder. We are busted or, more precisely, I am. We are taken back indoors and seated in a small bleak office. I don't know what it feels like to be in East Germany. It must be like this.

My brother looks miserable and scared. My heart plummets. Whatever I've brought on myself may be deserved but my brother's done nothing. Some managerial type says vaguely threatening stuff. He calls my parents, which is a strict drag. No police. I kind of wish I could trade my parents for the police. We get home, I assume on the bus, and when we arrive, I go into a sort of fugue state. I remember my parents arriving home and sitting on the bed in their room and nothing else. It's the South Portland house, though. That I remember.

The Pencil and the Magnifying Glass (1975)

I burn a pencil with a magnifying glass. I am lying on the rug in my parents' bedroom, which is not off limits. We have carpet everywhere, blue carpet, shit carpet. I have read somewhere that a magnifying glass can burn things. I don't know if this is true. I have a pencil and a magnifying glass. Later, somebody steals it. I wait and wait and burn off a little paint.

Copper Light (1990)

The flat copper light. Ten minutes later, the matte black of the bench is spiced orange by the paper-candle globes.

This book is like fish skin and the line of an opened can. I will read it again. The notebooks with the chocolate drums. I am with a new person and life feels like it has no sides, free and open and slightly unstable with joy. We are having the strangest moment in Virginia, though, staying on an actual plantation that has restyled itself as a prime conference venue. Most of the butlers are Black. I am trying to support Deborah on this work trip but I am losing the plot. I read Duchamp's journal and look at the chocolate drums.

Agata (2014)

Agata takes me to a forest outside Krakow, next to a zoo. We can touch the elephants without paying to go in. We walk and climb and walk and talk and eventually hold hands, the culmination of four days of sexual tension. This ends up being the entirety of our relationship. We return to the house where her lover, a sound engineer, is eating soup. She makes me tea. She has copies of eight different Biosphere CDs. When I get home to Brooklyn, we have a FaceTime conversation and she tells me, "We need to go to this festival," which seems to mean I need to get her into this festival. It occurs to me that our love might not be pure.

Skills (1985)

Skills are taught and loving me isn't a lesson. It is just my weather. It is very good weather. My parents teach me everything.

Tour Diary (1996)

Monday, May 20, NYC

The heat is record-breaking, ninety-six degrees, a good day for an office job with AC. I am not at my day job. Wilbo and I load out of my house on Lower Broadway and get caught at Canal and Centre streets, gridlocked. A traffic cop stands and watches. An eighteen-wheeler pulls into the intersection, blocking everything. The cop stares at the truck. I wonder what someone would pay me to stare at trucks. The heat has overpowered ConEd and there are brownouts blooming all over. We hear this on the radio the next day; in daylight, the lack of electricity is invisible. For the moment, our elevator doesn't work. That's no hardship for people with a few staircases to climb. Our gear modifies those feelings. Two bass players are a shipping nightmare.

Tuesday, May 21, NYC

Canal Street is wide and merciless, full of turbid commerce that makes *cheap* and *dirty* feel like Victorian euphemisms. Sometimes, all four corners of the Broadway and Canal intersection are sandbagged with garbage that raises a halo of stink above the lights. I don't mind. I wonder what powerful people think. We are on the edge of Chinatown and everyone is selling something. What about the German tourists looking down at their dog-eared maps? Do they come to New York for that smell? Maybe sellers are selling more because people want to jet through the smell—the echt experience of shopping for fake bags.

There was once a certain kind of vendor who rented a legitimate storefront and conducted business during daylight hours. These stores served a customer that no longer exists. It was once feasible that a civilian would make something for himself, using some combination of piping, mylar, paint, markers, police lights, resistors, capacitors. (The first plague to hit these businesses was the construction of the World Trade Center, when dozens of amateur electronic-supply stores were wiped out by the footprint of the construction.) The custom of these stores was rooted in the ways of a cohort of self-sufficient people who produced as often as they consumed. They're gone, as are the stores.

Around these ghosts stretch a loose, grey perimeter of people hawking copies of youth effluvia. If an item is a visual or audible good, it has been reproduced and made available on Canal Street for five dollars, next to pink-bronze switchblades, generators, plastic tubing, India ink, car stereos, old rocket launchers, porno, shish kebab, postage stamps (a block from a post office), imitation Gucci watches, fireworks, fried duck, and fried anything. The tinkerers and the bootleggers have both been pushed out by banks and hotels and restaurants you already have in your town.

That night at Irving Plaza, before show time, the security guy at the dressing room door stops everyone. It doesn't matter if we have laminates and wristbands—everyone is grilled. Nobody is there and nothing is happening. No matter. One man, stage left, is especially pleased to be unpleased with us. I imagine him walking around his backyard, wearing a vest with lots of extra pockets, timing response speeds as he loads and unloads and pulverizes skeet.

Wednesday, May 22, Carrboro, NC

We see little of Carrboro because we drive all day and arrive just in time for sound check. This is what any band will say about any town they've played on a tightly scheduled tour. During the show, someone reacts happily when Wilbo changes basses and fills the gap by mentioning he's from Trenton. We meet another veteran of tomato pies (underrated), steel rope, and pork roll.

Thursday, May 23, Atlanta, GA

We see a small burnt-out wooden building amidst the business towers as we drive in. We can't get a read on what part of town we're in. Dying commercial? Transitioning? After the show, we carry out fifteen bottles of raspberry-flavored "summer" beer. It occurs to me fifteen minutes out of town that we need to make sure these beers were not given in lieu of something we needed more, like money.

Ice Cream Sword Guy (1981)

The man cuts off the top of his ice cream with a sword. Why not get a small cone, one with ice cream only in the wafer stem? "She's busy," he says.

Kraze 12 (1982)

Kraze 12 does not bomb or tag. I practice throwing a perfect *A* or flicking out the tines of an *E* with my felt-tip pen. I do not tag. I cannot be a toy if I do not tag so I make cassette-tape liners with my constricted handstyles. Graffiti matters to me, deeply. John Cullum and I, boarding trains and studying the tags of the day. All I can come up with, as my offering, is this one tag—Kraze 12. The letters are balanced well enough, and the lines have some lift, some proportion. When it is time to fill out the letters and create a "piece" (short for masterpiece), I am less accomplished. I can make big boxy capital letters look good but I don't have the cartoonist's draftsman chops or the psychedelic noodler's patience. I just want to get the letters right, so I settle for the tape liners and posters and having impressive notebooks full of lists, which I still have.

I think the skills we end up turning into vocations are simply the things we can do for a long time without complaining.

I Don't Like Discos (1998)

In May of 1998, I give a talk at the Fuse 98: Beyond Typography conference in San Francisco. I have no business being there—my brother has finagled me an invite. I give a talk on the dangerous surfeit of possibilities presented by nonlinear digital recording software like Pro Tools. I call it "Too Many Knobs." The organizers find this pun too crude, so the title is changed (to what, I can't remember). I get to see my brother speak, which is fun. I also see David Carson speak.

The highlight, for me, is the fact that Panasonic are scheduled to play. (They have not yet been forced to change their name.) I meet Russell Haswell at the conference and walk about with him a bit. He wears a tracksuit jacket and uses the word "diamond" repeatedly, for anything he thinks is not terrible. I like him immensely.

Before the scheduled show, Panasonic become unscheduled: customs has seized their gear. The oscillators they use at the time are military-ish green boxes with huge Bakelite knobs, made in Russia and covered with Cyrillic. Since these items look "like weapons" to the airport authorities, they will not be released.

In Russell's company, I meet the band at the club they are supposed to be playing. Ilpo and Mika are below dead-pan. They don't smile or speak. In their stead, Haswell plays a set on MiniDisc.

I encounter lots of abrasive noise after 1998 without ever hearing another set like the one Haswell plays that night. I don't have recollections of sounds as much as impressions tied to images: wedges of aluminum and glass, stacked up like plates, rotating into each other, creating a range of high-pitched noises. His set suggests that the number of unpleasant, high-pitched noises is much larger than previously known. Russell gets around up there in those plates.

Everyone leaves, except for ten people. Neither member of Panasonic has said anything. About half an hour into Haswell's set, Mika turns to me and says, "I don't like discos." That is the only thing I ever hear him say.

Stasis (2013)

I think of my father and I cannot find the words. I don't know what to call my feelings or thoughts. I am not, it turns out, having feelings. I am not thinking. Nothing is happening.

Grief isn't pain—it's stasis. The heart seizes when time seizes. Time is what the heartbeat divides. When it shuts off, you can't tell if it's going to kick back on. You don't know if you'll recognize the rhythm when it comes back. Will you be able to hear yourself and know that you're alive? Is that same person still alive? Are you?

What brings on grief is a thing that will not change, a fact that doesn't bend under force. That information is harder than bone or wire and larger than a building. It is a loss and it does not move.

Grief is the sound we make when we run our hands across the surface of loss, something without bumps or divots. We nestle against it as if we were the ones testing its weight. Grief is the loop of our remembering when we found the wall. It is the sound an addict hears, a tinnitus of relief that never comes. We relive the encounter because we want to change the ending. We don't—the signal retains its shape. We play it again.

Kissing on the Promenade (1983)

In junior year, the main student drama production is *Romeo and Juliet*. My playwriting teacher, Nancy Fales-Garrett, is directing. The process of putting on the play begins (but does not end) with absolute drama. Nancy has already cast Juliet—Mia Sarapochiello is going to play the terminal goth lovergirl. You would cast Mia, too. She is unearthly, a Sargent painting who eats in the cafeteria. I am cast as her father, Capulet. There is an appropriate outcry. How can Nancy cast the biggest role without letting people try out for it? So there is a second Juliet, Margaret Sundell. Margaret and Mia are spot-on in different ways. Mia captures the descending weight of the story, the glacier of love melting into consciousness of horror, and Margaret conveys all the native pain and frustration. More productions should trade off leads within a single production. It becomes a lenticular play, different every other night.

Mia and I become close, which is a thrill for a boy beginning to wonder how to interact with girls. She ends up on *All My Children* in a small but consistent role. I occasionally drop her off at her house, which is right next door to my friend Ben Schwartz's house. We talk and flirt and remain tight. As far as the grace of human interactions go, it is lucky for me that our time together is so unfraught. She's just kind and we crack up a lot and I don't worry about it too much. It's helpful to have a play, which is an easier and healthier target for us to worry about. I'm afraid I'm going to be blown off the stage by everyone else. My best friend, John Cullum, runs off with the role of Mercutio, which gives me a jolt of bitterness, though it doesn't last. He's so perfect for it and I get Capulet's "chop logic!" speech. I'm always being cast as old men. The production is charged with optimism. I cannot imagine, at this very early point, that I will do anything other than theater. Why would I? Theater involves language and live performance, and plays have more teeth than anything on TV. The sets are pretty cheap and easy to make. Seems legit.

One night, Mia and I are walking near the Promenade. I am thinking about the music of her name—Sarapochiello. It's long and liquidy and sharp. It's like an identity you would design for yourself rather than a name you would inherit. The fall afternoon has gone dark and we are walking slowly. There's a bench, right there on Columbia Heights, so we sit next to each other. I slump against the guardrail and slide to the left. She arches over me and covers us with her jacket. We kiss, lightly, for a long time. I go somewhere that is not Brooklyn Heights and it is not bad.

We haven't begun a romance or embarked on a quest together. We are two kids stumbling across a pile of glass. There is no other move. You have to stop and look at a gathered pile of green-gray auto glass and you also have to stop and make out on the bench when it is time. I float down Columbia Heights to our apartment on Old Fulton Street.

John begins dating Mia almost immediately and they have a passionate first romance for several years. This, far from a disappointment, is a relief. I am not ready for anything beyond this and now that I have had the perfect kiss, I can enjoy that and not worry for a bit. For reasons I cannot explain, I never see *Ferris Bueller's Day Off*, though I do see every single episode of *AMC* that Mia is in.

Reel to Real (1980)

My first time playing music in a rehearsal studio is a frustration, a sour awareness that I am wasting money on something I don't know how to do. I expect to get together with my friends in a room and experience liftoff, cohesion, revelation, communal explosion. No. I just learn exactly how little I have learned. It isn't fun. And we aren't good. But I hear something.

My friend John and I spend days coming up with a band name. This is one of the things you do before you have a band. You think about a name, which is the last thing anyone outside the band cares about. For you, in the nonexistent band, the name kicks off ideas and gives you a persona, an idea of who you are playing, as a band. You need to fool yourself that you are important enough to do an improbable thing and a name is one step in a series of self-delusions you need to maintain the band. You think a name matters to the audience because that word is usually quite big on an album cover, and grows huge in the mind of a fan. The audience, though, generally doesn't care what the word is. (Did I care that I hated the word *Buzzcocks*? Not at all.) So we have Reel to Real. *R-e-e-L* to *R-e-a-l*. We switch the homonyms back and forth, like reels. I don't know which we chose. It's a bad name in any order. I'm fairly sure the words are in my head because of a lyric I can't place.

The plan is this. Because John has a Korg synthesizer, which is unusual for a thirteen-year-old, he will play keyboards. I will play a new black-and-white Rickenbacker guitar my godfather has purchased for me. My friend from the block over, Cinque Lee, will play drums. Another friend, Ben Chinitz, comes along as a witness or fake roadie or self-contained peanut gallery. Cinque's friend, Jamie Haft, who is the only kid at school who might be considered a bad kid—capital *B*, capital *K*—who throws a chair down the stairwell, will play bass. I have no idea that he owns a bass, but he does. We all go to school together.

I don't know who finds the studio. We probably look it up in the phone book because we are thirteen and have no connections to any bands, and where else would we look? It is somewhere near Jay Street in downtown Brooklyn, along an anonymous stretch. The block is the kind of place your parents drag you to for a terrifying civic moment, like filing for bankruptcy, which we have done. The stores that aren't closed on Saturdays sell bad clothing for too little and army gear for too much. Most of the buildings are flat cream, the color of file folders. These surfaces say I am permanently unfiled, that Brooklyn is always going to be lost and anonymous and disconnected from the colorful madness of Manhattan, the place where things matter and are written about.

We walk into the studio and the manager looks at us, unpleasantly surprised. It is dark. I think to myself that the carpet is like the carpet in a whorehouse, an idea that feels like a thought I am supposed to have. The carpet was once red and has elements that were once beige, all of it now a dried effluence hemmed by pine wainscot. The studio makes rent on classical quartets and voice-overs but we are the ones who walk in on that Saturday. The session costs us thirty dollars. I still have a pulpy receipt crossed with the dusty blue of duplicated handwriting. The bill is for either two or four hours. It feels like four. Or eight. Thinking of how thirty likes to divide, it is probably a bill for two.

What I learn from this session is not what I had expected to learn. There is a tape of the rehearsal. When I get home, I play it. The sounds resemble no music I hear on the radio, or any music I want to be associated with. I hear arguments and the clumsy touching of instruments. The tape dissuades me from trying to be in a band for a long time. Eventually, I go back to the tape. A few things emerge.

I hear four kids and their dumb friend screwing around. Why? Because somebody in the band needs an idea of what is going to happen, and nobody had one. The only person with organizational skills is our friend, Ben. He ordered a pizza, which came. We are not as productive. Over two hours, we try to play two songs: Gary Numan's "Cars" and Lynyrd Skynyrd's "Sweet Home Alabama." We choose "Cars" because John can play the melody on his synthesizer, and we play "Sweet Home Alabama" because I have sort of figured out the chords. Hearing the tape, it turns out I had no idea of how to get from one section to another, which makes knowing any single part useless.

What we are able to perceive, and recreate, is a motif. That bit is what makes a song a hit, and it's also a phrase that can be sampled. This moment is enough to evoke the whole song in a couple of seconds, with room for grain and character. If you know what comes next, or can improvise, the motif can bring out the rest of the music. Sampling is a few years away and simple, phrase-based music is ancient, so we aren't in some sort of magical sweet spot. What happens, accidentally, is that my experience of trying to be in a band sets me up to understand a technology that will then produce a new form while I am failing to master the existing form. I fail my way into an epiphany.

There are expensive synthesizers that can sample noises as early as 1976 but the first affordable units, drum machines that can store a few seconds of material, appear in the mid-eighties. And these motifs are all you can fit into a sampler, making them native to the machine in a way that long string passages can't be. The choice is made for musicians, because of the memory capacities in these machines, devices being developed just as we are rehearsing for the first time. But technology makes the artistic choices first.

This does not make our incompetence visionary. We are not intense and bad like punk. We want to duplicate known, hit recordings. We are a bad band, with a lesson in that badness. Our inability to get beyond phrases sets us up for the biggest revision yet of pop, which will loop these phrases.

That day, in 1980, we also forget that songs have an order, which is what makes them songs. Later, when I start writing music and being in a band, I see song shapes. I realize I need that skill, the ability to generate a map, if not a traditional score: an ordinal series of cues. It is easy to map the songs I write. Other people and their songs are another matter. Old blues records became touchstones partially because they are legible. Now, pop music is often beautiful because it is indeterminate. In 1980, though, great pop music has little use for indeterminacy or guys who can't play a song all the way through.

It is obvious when we start playing that we think playing riffs, individually, will cause the other guys in the band to fill out the song as it goes, as if riffs are generative pairs that have the DNA of an entire song built into them. Maybe if we push them together, like magnets, a form will appear. But, no, you all have to agree on what you are going to do and when, and how long the parts will last. As a job for hyperactive thirteen-year-olds, alignment is out of the question. Most of the rehearsal tape is us playing at the same time, for no more than thirty seconds, rarely in unison. We stop a lot, and laugh. Sometimes we figure out a transition, and suss out what the next part should be, but no song makes it to song-hood, and no single take makes it from the introduction to the chorus. We do better with "Cars" because it is centered on keyboards, and we can tag along after John. No matter—we always crack up, though I'm sure John knows the song. I think, for a moment, John tries to sing "Cars," but it is not on tape.

"Sweet Home Alabama" is full of singing. Singing appears to be important in pop songs, yet this is something none of us has bothered to think about. Who will sing the words? Did we assume a singer would be there, for us, like a bathroom? This may be one reason I end up in an instrumental band. I have the traumatic experience of being presented with music and having no idea of how to sing a song or find someone to sing it, coupled with the realization that our work will not make a song without singing. It does not occur to me that I can sing the song. The four of us only play together this one time. I don't know if we pretended that we would ever play together again.

Many bands operate under the illusion of being a collective because, in general, people don't like being told what to do, especially when they know that you can't play the instrument they play. But in an ideal situation, where nobody particularly wants to be the leader, a curious thing happens. People become skilled enough that they can play and remember what they play. You can write a song collectively without ever talking about it. The parts are in your body and that's where they stay.

Not many musicians like postperformance notes. In bands, there's a mystical imperative to not talk about what you're doing. You're supposed to figure it out, by yourself. If you point to what someone's done, it inches into the territory of baseball superstition. You've dared someone to look down and lose the magic. If something is off, noting that out loud is a personal attack. When someone's pitching a no-hitter, you don't mention it. If things are going badly, you talk even less.

Terrible moments are analogous to a relationship clog. You hit an impasse and know that the music has become boring, that something else is supposed to happen. But who will raise a hand? Who will say, "We are lost"? Nobody. You get coffee and move on.

Radio hits are produced in the opposite manner. Though they hit bumps, they are worked over mercilessly. The goal is not the same as writing a song that sounds like a band. The goal is to write a song that sounds, before anything else, like another song. The chances are good that someone in the room has already been paid. These people are imagining a car and they fix it as they build it. Bands, though, want to build vehicles that don't exist. This fact doesn't give preference to cars over future space mobiles but rather acknowledges that one process can't produce the other kind of vehicle.

At thirteen, we have no idea how records are made. Sometimes it turns out that the artists in question, those that resemble a band, haven't done the work, and instead have used producers and writers and other assistants. They are part of the car factory. But I fall into the impression, which I later stop caring about, that great bands are full of people who somehow bounce off of each other and create something without interference. That will be, every time, better than a known car. This is not the case, though. If you've ever been in a shitty spaceship, you know the value of a Camry. In all cases, though, success is correlated with a short motif that sticks. Maybe for one cohort, the motif will be submerged under noise and feel different than the anchor of a teenpop hit. Really, bands turn out to be looking in the same direction as the carmakers.

My life would be different if, on that day at the Jay Street studio, we had walked in and John had said, "Just follow me guys," and sang us through to completion. Maybe I would have thought, "Oh, the lead singer is the guy who figures it out." But I saw a bunch of guys, looking at each other, and not knowing what to do.

Punk (1977)

There are street fairs fairly often in Fort Greene. For one, I dress up as Ace Frehley from the cover of the third Kiss album, *Dressed to Kill*. The four band members are standing together near the corner of Twenty-Third Street and Eighth Avenue, all wearing dark three-piece suits and full face makeup. Unlike Halloween, where this would matter, my mom helps me assemble a little suit equivalent, which is authoritative and weird and perfect. She nails the makeup, too. Why this day of all days? I don't know. I'm glad she came through.

Once out on the street, though, context defeats me. The population around me is almost entirely Black and

Latinx. Then, I would have said, "Black and Puerto Rican." Everyone who seems vaguely Latino is called "Puerto Rican" in the seventies. I did not make these rules.

We have the swinging half-moon metal terror truck, where people are loaded into a *c*-shaped rack of metal benches and swung violently back and forth and high into the air. We have a bouncy castle, candy apples, souvlaki— the standard seventies fare.

There's a girl on my block named Celia whom I have a massive crush on. She has a perfect tiny face and a little mole and she is wearing jeans and a striped shirt. She curses almost all the time. I decide to ask her to go on a ride with me. Very few other kids at the fair are wearing makeup. Hm.

"No! You look like a fucking punk!"

That's the beginning, middle, and end of my date with Celia.

Paler (2007)

ME: hey sup

THEM: yes hello

ME: i have this idea about Dr. Dre and Nirvana and 1993

THEM: how does it relate to now?

ME: i guess everything is connected because, time

THEM: but like who is it about?

ME: well, before 1993, things were different. somebody like the clash were a great example of genre and race collision but that kind of un-self-conscious use of Black culture couldn't happen again. culture is impolite and brilliant and stupid and exceptional all at once. you could only be the clash and be the clash, if you get me, and that's not a theory! I could hardly hang an essay on that because what happened with snoop I mean I am not sure that is just spitballing

THEM: but ok who is the clash now

ME: i think the point is that we don't have one and can't have one now because we are more aware of appropriation and—

THEM: yeah but like a big band

ME: no i get it i just think—

THEM: like arcade fire

ME: they're definitely big and I like them but I think—

THEM: so like we show the "what if" by considering them

ME: but they're not trying to be the clash

THEM: that's the point

ME: no, it's much more about dre and kurt and the moment people tried to redefine the lanes people could stay in and—

THEM: but they have a big lane, arcade fire, and that's because of all that, right?

ME: sort of? I mean, a lot of things happen to create the conditions for any band

THEM: but race is at the front of all of this right?

ME: often but not always

THEM: we just need a peg

ME: ok

THEM: so arcade fire then

ME: i'll try it but this seems more like it's about a moment in the past

THEM: that's hard for an essay like this

ME: but i haven't written the essay yet

THEM: it just feels like one of those classic fight pieces

ME: ok wait hang on

THEM: you gotta be ready for those

ME: oh I am

THEM: I like the way you're thinking

ME: wait

The Mile Run (1977)

Springtime brings an atypically athletic competition to school. Students run competitively, racking up miles. Since the school has no large sports facility of its own, we run through Cadman Plaza Park. Some authority figured out how many laps are equal to a mile. You can be awarded a pin badge for running one, two, three, four, or five miles. The five-mile badge is red and I am embarrassed that I earn only one. I never turn down an opportunity to do a sporting thing, even if I have no deep passion for touch football or the varieties of stoopball that mostly involve running into traffic.

The Horseshoe (2019)

Drinking is like diving into a bell. The limits are severe. You are more or less banging your head on the same wall as you drink more.

The Summer of Knives (1983)

The summer of knives begins in June of 1983. At this point in St. Ann's history, the senior dance is held in commercial clubs and lofts, not at the school. Back in my sophomore year, in June of 1982, it was held in a duplex club somewhere in the meatpacking district. It was mysterious and wild and had a colored dance floor like the one you see at 2001 Odyssey in *Saturday Night Fever*. I was deliciously and immensely stoned and happy that night and had no idea where I was. I've never figured out what that club was.

My junior year, in June 1983, the senior dance takes place in a massive loft in the garment district, somewhere in the west twenties. It is a huge empty space and the vibe is not fantastic. I wander around, wishing the music was way louder, drinking beer out of cans, bored and happy and alone and free. John Gulla, the stocky math teacher who'd taught me in sixth grade, is manning the door. I have no idea how he figured out who was or wasn't allowed to get in; in retrospect, it seems this part of the event was not thought through. Gulla has words with some kid who then comes back and stabs him with a big kitchen knife. He lives, thank god. When we come back to St. Ann's in the fall, he shows us the scar running from his neck down to his pants. He becomes the head of the middle school about ten years later.

My drug use only happens on weekends and is, all in all, unimpressive. I never buy anything—my friends Alex and Sebastian, who live in Flatbush, buy "black beauties," which are not black beauties, and weed, which is weed. Things become codified the following year but during junior year, things are just getting going.

There are three different club music events that feel dreamlike, and one of them is the unknown light-up dancefloor spot. The other is more important. A dance party happens in Manhattan; even though there is a DJ and a bar, the room seems to be somebody's apartment or office on the third floor of an apartment building. Seb and Alex are there with me and they don't particularly like the music. I am in heaven.

On Friday nights, we get together at Alex's house and smoke weed and read *Zap Comix* while listening to Sabbath and Deep Purple and Zeppelin. I bring my tapes of Mr. Magic and Afrika Islam shows, which they let me play for maybe fifteen minutes. They do like "The Message" and some of the Furious Five stuff.

At the Manhattan party, I hear the DJ play "Sex Machine," which I'd never heard before. Alex and Sebastian head for the hallway and I am frozen. I slowly look over the dancers, in space, with my eyes, to the DJ, whom I think I can connect with. This does not happen. As "Sex Machine" ends, another song begins. It's rap, which is unusual to hear out in clubs. It has a wobbly keyboard bass line and hits slowly, with confidence. The voices are happy and slick and on the beat. I move through the crowd and reach the DJ. He can't hear me when I ask what the song is, so I stare at the revolving record. He holds up the generic Enjoy! Records sleeve, which is red with the word "Enjoy!" in a goofy silver serif font, like a shoe store bag. The label spinning around says "The Body Rock" but I can't see the artist's name, which seems long. I join my friends and we take more fake speed and drink Ballantine forty-ouncers and smoke weed and play *Defender* at the Hotel Bossert. We all wear army jackets.

Blackout (1977)

I know it is a blackout because it is July and I am listening to Kiss's *Love Gun* and the turntable slows and stops. The album comes with a paper gun that makes a small noise when you hold it out and flick your wrist down. I don't know it's a blackout because I have never been in one and would not have known the word. We are living with the Wingates because we are between houses. Jim Wingate is the organist and choir leader at church. He has loaded a video game onto this early PC, early enough that it is just called a "computer." I play it as often as I can, before being yelled at. Jim also has Beta and VHS decks, both larger than his TV screen. Everyone in the family is friendly.

I know it is a blackout because we are watching *Columbo* and the TV dies. My mom says it is a brownout and I yell up the stairs. It is not a brownout.

Worrywart (1973)

My mother calls me a "worrywart." I'm stung. Worrying and thinking are one act lazily divided. A worrywart sounds like one of those filmy organic mutations the English delight in cataloging and cooking.

Salamanca (1996)

Deborah and I go to Salamanca, Spain. I ruin my favorite shirt with sardine oil and we have unprotected sex once. We return home and Deborah is pregnant with Sam.

Dance Tapes (1982)

In junior year of high school, someone gets the notion that I have enough records to make a dance tape. I want to, and I will, simply to hear my records played loudly enough that I'll find out what they really sound like.

Our dance is held in the lobby, on the second floor. It is a marble and stone area that is big enough, barely, for a dance. The sound is decent. I don't know where the speakers or amps come from. I sit on the edge of a desk in the reception area, listening to my sequence of songs unfold. People react honestly. Recordings do not shame anyone into dancing. Records are disembodied, and they are not people. Nobody feels like they're insulting a person by not dancing to a record. If songs don't work, a DJ sees it right away. This represents a layer of distance more interactions could include.

Toward the end of the night, I realize that not many of the boys are dancing. I have no plans to dance, but I've danced in my room to Trouble Funk and the Fearless Four. I walk out onto the floor and move. The music carries me and I feel an alignment, like I am both playing and hearing the music. Dancing near someone gives me a clue as to who that person might be when they're not dancing. After this dance, there isn't much chance of anything else distracting for me for a while. Playing and hearing music are inherently social acts to me, even if nobody else is around.

Work It Out (2012)

Speed people talk and heroin people talk and drinkers talk. Those who don't talk are those for whom it has not "worked out." It is not possible to find out why it hasn't worked out but it is very possible to figure out what people are looking for, if they are. If you have what they want, and keep standing there, that thing is no longer yours.

Haunting (2016)

What if anxiety, depression—all the charcoal—is just haunting? What if interventions and healings and fixings are nonsense? I start to wonder if the science of the brain is just the work of an electrician who keeps rearranging the lights leading up to the house, adding and subtracting sconces, doing all kinds of extensive decorative work on a house he never enters. Perhaps I am just weak. Maybe I just want to get some ghosts into my own narrative to make the loop more interesting.

My depression responds badly to investigation, as if it's a person in a house who will never answer the door. I am inside that house, with the depression. It arrives like smell, or appears on me, a piece of clothing I've put on reflexively. The blue-blackness is a sudden instance, never a growing sensation. It doesn't ramp up. It turns on.

There is no preface, exactly. If there is one trigger, there are twenty. The damp comes and goes in a kill-switch sequence. Certain events happen and then I am in it. Getting out is patient work, except I can't learn the knot. Each time, I play the variables again. Go for a run, blast that particular album, don't drink coffee. Do drink coffee.

Brooklyn (1977)

Brooklyn is founded around 1630 by Walloon and Dutch farmers, and named Breucklen. According to a report on the Fort Greene Historic District prepared by the NYC Landmark Preservation Commission in September of 1978, "[the] village developed slowly and even by 1790, two years after the New York State Legislature incorporated Brooklyn as a town, the population was only 1,603."

The Fulton Ferry arrives in 1814 and horse-drawn cars to the ferry make daily commutes to Manhattan quite feasible. As early as 1823, Brooklyn properties are getting hot as an alternative to overcrowded Manhattan, which, as late as 1850, extends no further than Twenty-Third Street. In the 1830s, other steam boats start offering rides and the commute gets easier. Brooklyn is incorporated as a city in 1834.

Wallabout Bay is the body of water alongside what is known as the Brooklyn Navy Yard. People settle inward from the water, so Wallabout, now a mixed-use stretch of emptiness mostly under the BQE, is one of the first areas in Brooklyn with a name. Now it is "the part north of Fort Greene and Clinton Hill, near the Navy Yard." And the Navy Yard is no longer a navy yard. The last time I go there is for a performance piece. The first part of Brooklyn to go residential is Brooklyn Heights, in the 1830s. Fort Greene is rural well into the 1800s, full of hills and forests.

Fort Greene is full of shantytowns in the 1840s and 1850s. At first, it is considered part of Clinton Hill and not called Fort Greene. In the late 1840s, Walt Whitman advocates for a park to be built where "the mechanics and artificers of our city, most do congregate." First called Washington Park, it is renamed after Olmsted and Vaux redesigned the joint in 1868. It is fashioned for the leisure of merchants and lawyers buying up the "handsome brownstones (drawing their architectural inspiration from England and Holland)" being built around the park.

Brooklyn starts as independent farmland and becomes a suburb of Manhattan, which is a big roast for all of us who thought we lived in some kind of radically detached outpost. When people say—in the 1990s, no less—that they have only been to Brooklyn to visit BAM, well, they are part of an historical trend. As excerpted by the Landmarks Preservation Commission, here is E. Idell Zeisloft in *The New Metropolis*, a book published in 1899:

> Brooklyn has always been an adjunct of the metropolis rather than a city with a complete civic life of its own, a dwelling-place for business folk and employees who possess moderate incomes, and those of greater means who abhor the feverish and artificial joys of modern Babel. It is a vast aggregation of home and family life, and of the social pleasures that appertain thereto. There is little to be seen in Brooklyn save the streets and avenues, hundreds of miles of them, filled with rows of

dwelling houses…. All of Brooklyn, indeed, with the exception of the waterside street and range of cloud piercing office buildings in the Civic Center area … is the exclusive domain of women and children during the daylight hours.

Developers offered homes with hand-carved ashlar masonry, intricate vestibule tile work, detailed marble and alabaster working fireplaces in every room, ground-floor kitchens and family dining rooms, parlor-floor studies and formal dining rooms with detailed foliate plaster work, master bedrooms, servants quarters, back-yards, etc.

In the 1950s, lawyers split for the new suburbs and Fort Greene fills up with boarding houses. When my family lives at 25 South Portland, the house next door is occupied by boarders. In the 1870s, the slums along Myrtle Avenue are filled with the Irish and their hogs, long before the weed stores and bodegas of the 1970s.

No Parents in the Stands (1977)

I don't want my parents coming to my baseball games. They come to one of the awards dinners and it makes me so nervous I go alone the next year.

Rainbow Room (1977)

My parents take me to the Rainbow Room for my tenth birthday. They have ordered a cake with King Kong depicted in icing. We see the Dino De Laurentiis remake of *King Kong* that night, because my great-grandfather wrote the story for *King Kong*. (He didn't write the script and died before the original movie was released.) The Rainbow Room turns us away because my brother, then seven, and I are minors. I don't understand how the restaurant doesn't know two children are having a birthday celebration that night, what with the cake. I don't understand how my parents don't solve this problem. As will happen over and over again, they confront a problem and throw their hands up. We come home, in our suit jackets, on the subway, carrying the cake.

The White Guy (1989)

In 1989, I am starting a new band and socializing with people who listen to the same music as I do. I watch Dee Barnes present videos on *Pump It Up!* and listen to rappers who believe in, or at least repeat bits of, Five Percenter philosophy.

In April of 1989, my friend Chuck Stone gets his first video job, directing the music video for Living Colour's "Funny Vibe." Vernon Reid's lyrics are an internal monologue, a series of responses to moments of everyday racism ("Why you wanna give me that funny vibe?"). Chuck illustrates the words with theatrical scenarios acted out by his friends. His friend Royal Miller plays the Black Man, scaring white ladies in elevators and not getting cabs. His friend Paul Williams works the stereotypes (basketball player, pimp, b-boy). I am the White Friend Who Acts Black.

Chuck is in the video, too. He goes by Charles now.

I don't think about how I should dress for the shoot. I just wear what I wear—a black leather jacket, a woolly winter hat, jeans, and creepers. It is cold as hell. My clothes don't convey a specific style, or the decision of someone who is trying to be part of a different cohort. I do not look like a member of 3rd Bass; I just look like a kid who types up surveys in Quark, which I am. The only thing I pull off is the "white" hand moves in the interstitials. Or maybe I don't—judge for yourself.

Then they make a second video! Prince Paul remixes the tune, and Daddy-O of Stetsasonic raps over it. Did the label want to see the band, who weren't in the original at all? But then why would they remix the song and make it worse?

Chuck asks me to be in the "What 'U' Waitin' '4'" video for the Jungle Brothers. This shoot is the inverse of "Funny Vibe." We rarely see Chuck. It is just three nerdy white dudes and two hundred Black teenagers in a Chelsea warehouse waiting around. Chuck recreates the *Soul Train* dance line. (I pop up for a moment at 3:36.) At one point, as the day wears on, Afrika Baby Bam gets up in my face (like, zero inches away) and raises his wooden staff to deliver a short speech about freedom.

I am very psyched when Chuck gets the "Bonita Applebum" video. He's already done the video for "I Left My Wallet in El Segundo," but artists weren't yet being loyal to specific directors. However much I like these other bands (which is a lot), that is nothing next to how I feel about Quest, even before *The Low End Theory*. Q-Tip has been showing up on De La Soul and Jungle Brothers tracks and already seems like he is hearing something weirder, both bigger and quieter. I am not in this video, though. I'm hoping this will be the outcome of all my extra work—falling down the stairs in a Quest video or maybe playing a cactus. Alas.

Pond (1976)

The magic of the pond, holding your body and leaving itself on you.

What The! (1998)

It's impossible to determine when or where I get the tinnitus. (Pronounced "TINN-i-tuss," because "tin-IGHT-us" would be a swelling of the tinn, which is not a thing.) There have been so many rehearsals spent next to the drummer's cymbals, so many gigs standing too close to the bass bin.

Videos in England (1980)

Videos are where I first see other people dance, because I can't go to clubs. I am thirteen. David Bowie's "Ashes to Ashes" is the first video I see, while staying at my grandmother's house in Kent, in the south of England. It is late 1980. I watch an entire cricket match because I get the notion that there might be a video after the match. What if I get up at the wrong moment and miss those four minutes? I wait and wait, with no plans of moving, simply because I see a snippet of some video ending as I arrive with my parents and I assume that videos only exist in England.

The World Famous Supreme Team's "Hey DJ" gives me an idea.

I see "Hey DJ" in 1984, a senior in high school. The clip is programmed into an hour-long show called *Friday Night Videos*. The Supreme Team is a pair of New York radio DJs who were scooped up by Malcolm McLaren and turned into recording artists, sort of. They are, more specifically, voices thrown on top of crushing, minimal productions like "Buffalo Gals" and "D'Ya Like Scratchin'?" as well as "Hey DJ," a more approachable track with actual piano playing and actual singing in the chorus. A song! The Supreme Team never become recognizable faces and barely make it out of 1984 before being resurrected in 1997 for Mariah Carey's "Honey," which really just wants the piano, not them.

The key part of the video is the introduction: four girls, appearing one by one and looking over their shoulders at the camera while playing video games, throwing out their hips and dancing in place. As dopey as this sounds, the fact that people dance to records is a surprising thing to see on TV. Videos barely exist and synchronized movement is not yet a staple of the genre. When I see this video, I remember that girls like dancing to records.

Can I Get a Diet Coke? (1995)

My father loves the people around him and is also unable to see his needs as anything other than incredibly urgent missions the people around him must complete. When I graduate from Columbia in 1993, his main line of commentary after the ceremony is that he has not brought enough trail mix. Then, walking east, toward the train station, my father turns to us and says, "Is there anywhere around here I could get a Diet Coke?" He is maybe thirty feet away from an Au Bon Pain, a national branch that is almost certainly familiar to him as a place where Diet Coke can be found. There is also the sharpened peak to the query, as if he has been deprived of Diet Coke for years. Third, and most relevant, is the fact that we have only just left the campus. The fact he has ended up in such a fragile state of dehydration and disorientation is very much my dad.

But his complaint isn't serrated like the demands of a real diva. He goes back quickly to being a team member after stamping his foot. My father is rarely in a bad mood. I almost always think of him in his seersucker jacket, smiling and walking with his briefcase-ish bag slung over his shoulder. I am fairly sure I equip myself for the day much as he did, with a certain weight of jacket and a certain satchel with a strap. It is likely that this was never any different. When I discover the Globe Canvas messenger bags in the eighties, I distinguish myself by a grand distance of a foot or two, the way kids do. I am going to be different but essentially as much like my dad as I can pull off. He has his nylon business sack well LISTEN HERE kids this is a MESSENGER BAG so back up.

I likely love him in ways I still don't understand.

Home (2017)

A huge percentage of people who talk about New York like experts only come to Times Square and draw their conclusions from this one visit.

Robyn + Brenda (2019)

The phrase I settle on is "club dancing." I don't think other people say this. For a long time, club dancing is my favorite way to get exercise and meet people and hear songs played at really high volume. In 1986, I fall in love with a woman named Brenda and this is what we do, as often as we can. Before we date, I don't speak to Brenda more than once. We end up at a party and instead of talking, we dance in front of a fireplace for hours. We are together for almost three years. We go to clubs in Manhattan like Madam Rosa and Hotel Amazon. When she falls in love with a woman named Julissa, I fall in love with a woman named Deborah, and that is that. We only see each other when someone dies, mostly on her side.

Club dancing is my early faith. It's frustrating, though. It has no fixed place. You have steps and moves, arranged in no particular order. It's not choreography and it's not undisciplined nonsense. You see it in shows like *Soul Train*, though it really happens later in the century than that. If two people are club dancing, they are dancing independently at each other. It feels like a specific historical formation, familiar to people who are now between thirty and sixty.

Brenda is not someone I think of lightly. She is close to my center and we don't do anything wrong other than be young and think we have to get married. (We do not.) Watching Robyn at Barclays Center recently, I think of

Brenda. I don't feel uncontrolled surges of raw sentiment. I feel warm and cared for, held in a strong and calibrated middle.

Boots and Roses (2010)

I go to Stockholm to interview Björk on stage in a theater, as part of her winning the Polar Music Prize. There are so many bouquets of flowers in the theater that it smells like an unrefrigerated flower shop. Björk tells me during the interview that Iceland is for boots, London is for trainers, and New York is for heels. That's what I remember from our interview. That night, the king of Sweden hosts a big dinner for Björk, attended by a zillion fancy people. I am told by someone there that if the king of Sweden remains seated, I, too, have to remain seated.

The dinner is about five hours long and the food is doled out in fourteen individual courses. I am seated next to a billionaire who is trying to fund an opera about the Holocaust which either does or doesn't involve Steve Reich. After several hours, I stand up to stretch. Of all people, Robyn, in platform sneakers, comes toward me. She thanks me for writing about her, and I say something half in English and half in—it is true—French. Yup. Your high school cafeteria nightmare. It gets both better and worse. I am still trying to recover from "Thank you, *beaucoup*—no, *vraiment*" when who saunters up but

Björk. I turn and before I can say something in Tagalog, these two cream-colored bots glide in and say, "The king is seated—wrap it up."

This is a good fifteen seconds.

Lego (2018)

We are a finite number of Lego pieces that can be rearranged in infinite ways. The idea that people can't change is a hideous distraction meant to immobilize.

Morning Coffee (2020)

A small rolling calm that is attracted to the edges of things.

2 Grove Street (1992)

Before Deborah Holmes dies on January 4, 2021, we have two sons and live together in four homes, three of which are apartments in Manhattan. When I'm near our first spot, on Sullivan above Houston, I think of *Twin Peaks*, which started airing while we lived there. We have two distinct friend groups in 1990, as you might expect from a dropout lawyer and a dropout dropout. This location never cues a ghost. Our second apartment, at the corner of Grove and Hudson, is kryptonite. We are in love there, two twenty-somethings in a tiny West Village one bedroom. We lay vinyl tiles in a kitchen that always smells of gas and I get fired from the Dustdevils while sitting in the living room and talking on a landline to the guitarist who had left and is returning to claim her old spot by doing her boyfriend's wet work. (He is too scared to fire me himself.) I buy cut-out CDs at a discount shop on West Fourth that's gone, though the Chase Bank next door isn't. Then, the loft. The boys live there now, at least sometimes. There are too many facts and failures and dreams in the air to be threatened by the fluid reality of the space: its reality is too vivid to be reduced. Two Grove Street is where the promise and youth and unresolved passion found a perch. It represents love and nothing else.

Me Myself and I (1988)

When the first De La Soul single comes out in 1988, I am twenty-one and working at Food. Downtown Records has moved uptown a few blocks to a spot on Twenty-Fifth Street, slightly east of Sixth. Rap records are stocked in wire racks, on the right wall, just as you enter.

One day, I pick up a single on the Tommy Boy label called "Plug Tunin'." It is by a group I've never heard of called De La Soul. I take it out of the racks because Tommy Boy is one of the labels that still puts out a fair amount of rap and not much else. "Plug Tunin'" is fucked up by any standard. The beat is too slow and too dirty. The main sample is a brass instrument, maybe a trumpet slowed down or a sped-up trombone. The rhymes are almost impossible to make out. Do the words even rhyme? Posdnuos—a name it takes me ages to figure out how to write—seems to be the leader, since he raps more. In his first verse or two, I can make out the word "paragraph," which I appreciate. The rest sounds like someone reading from a redacted FBI document, gaps as much as clauses.

I buy the next De La Soul single, "Me Myself and I," and I am a little surprised when it gets played on daytime radio. It is playing all the time at Food. The song is centered around a big chunk of Funkadelic's "(Not Just) Knee Deep." This kind of sample will soon be seen as a cheat—like "Super Freak" whaleboning "U Can't Touch This"—since the familiarity and catchiness of the original seems to be convincing the outliers. We are years away from the hip-hop authenticity wars. Rap fans are still trying to get people to stop making fun of rap. *Funkadelic? Great. De La Soul? We like them, so, whatever, this can work.*

The "Me Myself and I" twelve-inch is the only piece of vinyl like it I've seen: three-sided. The A-side is pressed like any other record, with one song following another.

The B-side is pressed with two interlocking grooves. One groove will play two mixes of "Me Myself and I," sequentially, while the other groove plays a completely different song. Which groove engages depends on where and how you place the needle. It is a kick and a pain in the ass and I probably try three times, maximum, before giving up on the B-side.

It doesn't matter that I don't love any of the sides of "Me Myself and I." I am generally in favor of rap becoming as user-unfriendly as the work of downtown types like Christian Marclay, who seems to be referenced every time somebody has to write about rap. Marclay hasn't made a record with interlocking grooves, so there! But what do I know? Maybe he has. I love his work, but I feel sides forming.

By 1989, I am working at Families & Work Institute—only three blocks away from Downtown Records—plotting the band that will become Ui, and flirting with a new hire named Deborah.

Acknowledgments

This book would not have been possible without the help of: Heidi DeRuiter, Sam Frere-Holmes, Jonah Frere-Holmes, Michael Miller, Joe Levy, Alex Ross, Elvia Wilk, Catherine Lacey, Molly Young, Léon Dische Becker, Scott Ponik, David Grubbs, James Hoff, Hua Hsu, Kiera Mulhern, and Lucy Teitler. Special thanks to Chris Kraus, Hedi El Kholti, Janique Vigier and Robbie Dewhurst for making this go into the world.

Sasha Frere-Jones grew up in Fort Greene, Brooklyn. His play, *We Three Kings*, was recognized by the Young Playwrights Festival in 1983 and performed at The Public Theater. He completed a short film called *The Take* in 1986. His first band, Dolores, completed two albums in the Eighties, and he is a member of Ui, whose work is available through The Numero Group. Frere-Jones plays with Body Meπa, who record for Hausu Mountain, as well as Calvinist and Fellas. He has written about music and books since 1994, and lives in the East Village with his wife.